FROM THE
NANCY DREW FILES

THE CASE: When someone with murder on the mind checks into the Old Pine Inn, it's up to Nancy to check out the suspects.

CONTACT: Michael Wentworth, president of the fraternity, set up the mystery weekend . . . but did he also set himself up for murder?

SUSPECTS: Jim Haines—The fraternity turned him down when he tried to join; now, as a handyman at the inn, he may be out to exact revenge. . . .

Trish Mays—She's Michael's ex-girlfriend and she's still obsessed by him; she may even love him to death. . . .

Matt Gervasio—Trish is using him to get to Michael; now, hurting Michael could be a way to hurt her. . . .

COMPLICATIONS: For Nancy and Ned, the whole idea of the murder mystery weekend was to spend time together. But while Nancy spends her time on the investigation, Ned seems to spend all of his trying to comfort Michael Wentworth's former and present girlfriends!

Books in The Nancy Drew Files™ Series

Available from ARCHWAY Paperbacks

THE
NANCY DREW FILES™

123

WICKED FOR THE WEEKEND

CAROLYN KEENE

AN ARCHWAY PAPERBACK
Published by POCKET BOOKS
New York London Toronto Sydney Tokyo Singapore

This book is a work of fiction. Names, characters, places and incidents are products of the author's imagination or are used fictitiously. Any resemblance to actual events or locales or persons, living or dead, is entirely coincidental.

AN ARCHWAY PAPERBACK *Original*

An Archway Paperback published by
POCKET BOOKS, a division of Simon & Schuster Inc.
1230 Avenue of the Americas, New York, NY 10020

Copyright © 1997 by Simon & Schuster Inc.
Produced by Mega-Books, Inc.

ISBN: 0-671-00748-3

First Archway Paperback printing October 1997

10 9 8 7 6 5 4 3 2 1

NANCY DREW, AN ARCHWAY PAPERBACK and colophon are registered trademarks of Simon & Schuster Inc.

THE NANCY DREW FILES is a trademark of Simon & Schuster Inc.

Cover art by Bill Schmidt

Printed in the U.S.A.

IL 6+

WICKED FOR
THE WEEKEND

Chapter

One

WHO SAYS I CAN'T win the contest?" Ned Nickerson asked, a determined expression on his face. Nancy Drew looked over at him and sighed as she maneuvered her blue Mustang down the winding country roads that led to the Old Pine Inn.

"I never said you *couldn't* win," Nancy teased. "I just said that you probably *wouldn't* win!"

Ned laughed and then leaned over and nuzzled Nancy's neck.

"Hey! Quit that or we'll get into an accident before we even get there," Nancy said, giving Ned a dazzling smile. She pushed her reddish-blond hair back from her face and adjusted the window to give her hair a break from the wind.

Although it wasn't quite five o'clock, the air was getting chilly, and Nancy was glad she'd

1

worn her leather jacket. Suddenly the warm early fall days seemed numbered, and Nancy noticed a difference—a new crispness and a shift in the light of the day—that marked the approaching change of season.

Nancy was excited about the upcoming event. Ned's fraternity, Omega Chi Epsilon, was hosting a weekend at the Old Pine Inn for the brothers and their guests. The inn held a variety of specialty events, and the fraternity had chosen the "murder mystery weekend." The first guest to identify the murderer and solve the mystery would win a prize. It promised to be an action-packed few days.

The action started a little sooner than Nancy had anticipated when a red convertible sports car raced right up to the back of Nancy's Mustang and hung there. "Do you know who that is?" Nancy asked Ned. Tailgaters always made her nervous.

Ned looked out the back window at the car behind them. "It's Number One," he said, using the nickname for the Omega Chi president, Michael Wentworth.

Michael hit the horn, then smoothly overtook Nancy's car. Nancy caught a glimpse of the couple inside. Michael's sunglasses hid his eyes, but there was no mistaking Omega Chi's president, with his chiseled face and million-dollar smile. "Who's the girl with Michael?" Nancy asked, glancing at the blond girl in the passenger seat.

"That's Mia Tyler, Michael's new girlfriend," Ned said absently, his concentration on the map he had open on his lap. "Okay, we'd better be watching now. The road to the inn should be coming up on the right."

When they rounded the next bend in the road, Nancy saw a sign pointing to their turn for the Old Pine Inn. About a quarter mile down the gravel drive, she spied the inn, an impressive Victorian building with turrets and gables. It was surrounded by dozens of stately pine trees. Off to the side was a swimming pool; a set of grass tennis courts was partially hidden by more trees.

Nancy parked the Mustang, and she and Ned carried their bags up the porch steps. Nancy envisioned spending some cozy moments with Ned in the comfortable rocking chairs that graced the wide, wraparound porch.

"This is great!" Nancy said as they stepped inside the lobby. Plush red carpeting and textured wallpaper made for a rich atmosphere, and a crackling fire in the parlor added to the Victorian charm.

"We'd better register before all the good rooms are taken," Ned said, pointing to the front desk. "There are a few single-occupancy rooms that are given out on a first-come, first-served basis," he explained, "and I don't want anybody snoring at me this weekend!"

They walked over to a desk in the lobby where a young woman checked them in and gave them keys to their rooms. "I love this place!" Nancy exclaimed as she and Ned walked up a wide staircase to the second floor. "I can't wait to see my room."

Nancy's room was bright and cheerful, with yellow flowered wallpaper and bedding to match. The window commanded a view of an expansive lawn that sloped down to a small lake. "This is beautiful." Nancy sighed.

Net set down Nancy's suitcase. "It's a little too flowery for me, but if you're happy I'm happy," he said, and gave her a kiss on the nose. They agreed to meet downstairs in fifteen minutes, and Ned went off to his room.

Nancy unpacked quickly. As she was leaving her room, she saw Mia Tyler struggling with an armload of books and trying to unlock the door next to her own.

"Hi. Here, let me help you," Nancy insisted, taking some books out of Mia's arms. "I'm Nancy Drew. Ned Nickerson and I saw you speed past us in the Michaelmobile."

"Hi! Thanks for the help," Mia said as she finally got the door open. "I brought my bag up earlier, then went out to the car to get my books and papers. I couldn't find a bellboy, and Michael has already disappeared with his buddies."

Nancy carried the books into Mia's room and

set them on a bureau. "I thought this weekend was for fun, not for schoolwork!"

"I know," Mia said, "but I can't afford to get behind." She blew her blond bangs off her forehead with a soft *phew*.

"Well, I hope you take some time off to enjoy yourself," Nancy said as she let herself out the door. "I guess I'll see you later."

"Yeah, okay," Mia said as she began arranging the books and binders into several piles. "Thanks again."

Nancy hurried downstairs to find Ned in the lobby, laughing and joking with a group of fraternity brothers. "Here's my winning ticket now," Ned said, reaching out to put his arm around Nancy's shoulder. "The world-famous detective, Nancy Drew, is going to help me solve the mystery and win that prize!"

"No way, Nickerson!" Nancy said. "No help from me on this one!"

The guys laughed. "Excellent! You'll be as clueless as the rest of us, Ned," said Matt Gervasio, a tall, blue-eyed Omega Chi and one of Ned's best friends.

"Come on, Ned," said Nancy before he could defend himself. "Let's take a look around outside."

Nancy and Ned took a long walk around the lake, then headed back up the spacious lawn, toward the swimming pool.

5

"It's cool to be here with the guys," Ned said. "But I'm really glad to be here with you."

"I know," Nancy said softly. "It seems like forever since we've spent any time together."

They sat on one of the lounge chairs around the pool, and Ned gave Nancy a long, lingering kiss.

Although Nancy lived only a couple of hours from Emerson College, she'd been busy and hadn't seen Ned for a few weeks. Her father, Carson Drew, was a prominent criminal lawyer in River Heights and had needed Nancy's help. And then when she'd been free, Ned had been busy trying to get a jump on the semester's workload. They always kept in touch by phone, but Nancy often found their conversations unsatisfying.

"You can't get one of these over the phone," Ned murmured, kissing her again.

"You read my mind," Nancy replied, glad that, as usual, their time apart hadn't cooled their relationship one bit.

They sat, talking quietly, until it was dark. "We'd better head in for dinner," said Nancy. "I'm starved, and the sample menu I saw in my room looked delicious."

Nancy and Ned went inside and found the dining room. Full-length windows graced with heavy draperies lined one wall of the grand room. Many of Ned's fraternity brothers and their dates were already seated, and the room hummed with conversation.

Michael saw Nancy and Ned and waved them over to his table. "Join us. Mia should be here any minute," Michael said. A moment later she arrived, and when Michael started to introduce the girls, Nancy told him they had already met.

"She's the one with all the books and no time for fun," Nancy said, smiling.

"I'll make sure she has fun this weekend—right, Mia?" Michael said.

"Tons of fun, Michael," Mia answered as she picked up her menu. "But you know I've got tons of work, too. We've talked about this before," she said, sounding exasperated.

"I know Mia seems very serious and very studious," Michael said to Ned and Nancy. "But deep down, under all those textbooks and study notes, is a girl who knows how to have a good time. She's actually the one who came up with the idea of holding our frat weekend here," he said with a tinge of pride.

They ordered dinner and talked, and Michael filled them in on the plans for the weekend. "What happens is, we watch an ongoing murder mystery play, and some of us get to join in the action," he said.

"And to the victor go the spoils," said Ned. "Victory is mine, with Nancy on my team."

"Sorry, bud, I told you before—you're on

your own," Nancy said, trying to hide her smile. "Besides, who says I don't want to win the prize myself?"

"Oh, great," Ned said, feigning dejection. "Never mind then. How about we heighten the stakes?" he asked, raising an eyebrow. "Care to place a friendly wager just between the two of us?"

"You're on, Nickerson," Nancy said. She looked up to see a waiter bringing their dinners. "But since we don't even have a single clue yet, let's eat!" Everyone laughed.

Once the food was served, Michael ate a few bites, then excused himself to make a phone call back to the fraternity house. A few minutes later Mia also excused herself.

As she ate Nancy looked around the elegant dining room. Nancy recognized nearly all the Omega Chis and some of their dates. At a table in the corner, however, sat four people—two men, an elegantly dressed woman of about fifty, and a striking redheaded girl who looked to be about Nancy's age.

Just as Nancy was about to ask her friends if anyone knew the women, the innkeeper, Mrs. McVee, entered the dining room and asked for everyone's attention.

"Welcome to the Old Pine Inn," she began, "and to our special murder mystery weekend. There will be several rounds of action, during which actors in character will reveal things about themselves and about each other. Pay careful attention. You'll be given opportunities to ask questions of the players, and you do not have to share your findings with other guests. Remember, it's a competition to the finish! Please notice the schedule of scenes posted in the lobby. Don't miss any, or you'll severely limit your chances to win a special prize. Now enjoy your dinner, and let's begin!"

Ned smiled fiendishly at Nancy. "Remember, Drew, a competition to the finish!"

"You don't have to—"

Nancy was interrupted by the older woman she had noticed earlier, now speaking in a loud stage voice.

"Hello, excuse me. Yes, hello," the woman said, looking around the dining room. "Whenever I stay at the Old Pine Inn, I like to meet my fellow guests; it's such an intimate setting. I'm Mrs. Katherine Wendham, and this is my daughter, Olivia," she said, placing a hand on the redheaded girl's arm.

Ned leaned in to Nancy's neck to whisper. "So the players are supposedly guests, too?"

"Oh, you're quick, Ned," Nancy whispered back, teasing.

"This is Derek Waverly, my late husband's business partner and a friend of the family," Mrs. Wendham continued, smiling at the handsome, dark-haired man at her table who looked to be in his early forties. Although he was well-dressed, Nancy thought his clothes seemed slightly out of date.

"And sitting beside Olivia is Robert Jones," said Mrs. Wendham, beaming at a young man Nancy thought was probably twenty. He smiled nervously, revealing a pronounced overbite, and pushed his eyeglasses up onto the bridge of his long nose. Olivia visibly squirmed during this last introduction.

"Robert," said Mrs. Wendham. "I'm so pleased you could join us this weekend. Olivia is delighted, too, aren't you, Olivia?" she added, looking sharply at her daughter, who rolled her eyes.

"Jeffrey!" Mrs. Wendham called. Immediately a tall, stooped man in his late sixties entered the dining room and walked toward Mrs. Wendham as briskly as he could manage. "Yes, Jeffrey. Would you take this plate away, please?" She turned to the guests. "Although I'd never say so to Mrs. McVee, I find I have to bring my own butler if I want to be sure to have the attention to which I'm accustomed."

Just then another woman rushed into the dining room. She was wearing a stylish outfit in rich autumn tones and a crushed velvet hat. She looked to be in her early twenties.

"Mickey Sloan," announced Mrs. Wendham. "Late for dinner, but never late on a deadline for one of her society-page nonsense columns."

Mickey Sloan didn't sit with the other actors.

Instead, she joined Nancy's large table and sat beside Ned. Nancy noticed in particular her intense green eyes.

"Well, I guess that's everyone," said Mrs. Wendham. "I look forward to talking with all of you throughout our stay this weekend, but now I need to see to some personal business. Robert, could you join me, please?" Jeffrey helped Mrs. Wendham from her chair, and the three of them walked out of the dining room. The remaining actors continued a staged conversation.

"At last, I am alone with the lovely Olivia Wendham!" Derek Waverly said in a joking manner.

"Please, Derek, you're wasting your time on me," Olivia said, putting down her fork. "My fiancé will be here any minute!"

"I'm sure your mother didn't invite him this weekend," Derek said, grinning slyly.

"That's true, but I'm hoping the information he's bringing will make Mother see that intelligence and honesty are more important than money. She'll just have to accept that I'm in love with him and that he's the one I'm going to marry," Olivia declared as the doorbell rang faintly in the distance.

"What could he possibly say that will change your mother's mind? She obviously wants the wealthy Robert Jones for you," Derek said as Olivia stood up from the table.

Olivia stopped and looked Derek Waverly in

the eye. "Either way, that lets you out, Derek. Not that I'd ever be interested in a man who is way too old for me, can't swim, can't dance, and doesn't know how to party. Besides, Michael told me he's bringing information that will lead to the thief who stole Mother's diamonds!" She dashed out the dining room door.

Nancy and Ned turned to each other and playfully gasped as the crime was revealed. Ned put his arm around Nancy's shoulder as they turned their attention back to the drama.

Derek Waverly was now alone at the table. "I wonder what kind of evidence that boy could have found," he said, as if to himself. He stared after Olivia for a moment, then rose and followed her out. Mickey Sloan, too, got up from where she sat at Nancy's table, saying she wanted to get her pen and pad from her bag in the lobby.

Olivia reentered, and following close behind her, to Nancy's amazement, was Michael Wentworth! He stole a quick grin at his friends in the dining room before turning to Olivia.

"I found an important lead, Olivia. And what I have to tell you is going to be quite a shock." A smattering of applause and a couple of catcalls from the fraternity brothers heralded their friend's debut, breaking the mood briefly.

At that moment Mrs. Wendham returned to the dining room. "What are you doing here?" she said to Michael. "I told you to leave Olivia alone!"

"I asked Michael here, Mother," she said. "He has some information."

"What information?" asked Mickey Sloan as she entered the room carrying a notepad. "Is it about the diamonds? That's it, isn't it? Olivia's fiancé knows who took them!" she said. "What a great story this will make!"

Mrs. Wendham glared at Mickey. "There won't be any story," she said. "Michael was just leaving."

"No, not yet," Olivia pleaded. "Why don't we all have some tea and calm down?" She took Michael's hand and led him to the table.

"No, I've had enough of this," Mrs. Wendham said. "I'd prefer to have my dessert with Mrs. McVee. Olivia, I expect your guest to be leaving shortly." She turned to leave the room and took Mickey by the arm. "Why don't you join me?" she asked, leading her out the door.

"I'm sorry about your mother, Olivia," Michael said. "But I had to see you today. Wait till you see what I've found. . . ."

His voice trailed off when Jeffrey entered the room with a tea tray and put it on the table.

"Thank you, Jeffrey," Olivia said as the butler left the room. She fixed two cups of tea and handed Michael a cup. "Milk, no sugar, right?" she asked him. Michael nodded and took a big sip from the cup.

"Michael is doing a terrific job, isn't he?" Ned whispered to Nancy. She nodded. "Maybe he

13

should skip medical school and take up acting!" he added.

Olivia was looking intently at Michael. "We're alone now," she said. "What do you have?"

"This," Michael said, reaching into his pocket and pulling out a crumpled bit of newspaper. As he dramatically held it out to Olivia, his hand began shaking. He dropped the paper onto the table. "But I need to explain . . ."

"Look, Ned," Nancy whispered, pointing to Michael. "He looks kind of funny."

Suddenly pale, Michael was wiping his forehead with a napkin. He picked up his teacup, but his hand was shaking so badly, he dropped the cup, and tea sloshed all over the white tablecloth. Then he grasped his throat with both hands and moaned.

Olivia sprang toward him. "Michael!" she cried. "What is it?"

Michael turned his gaze to Olivia. "The tea," he choked, pointing to the tray on the table. "I think I've been poisoned!"

Michael collapsed in the chair, his body half sliding onto the floor. Olivia lightly slapped his cheeks, trying to get him to come around. "Michael," she whimpered, "please, wake up!"

The guests sat silently, intently watching the action. The overhead lights in the room slowly brightened, changing the mysterious mood and signaling the end of the scene. "Dessert and coffee in the front parlor," Mrs. McVee called.

People now started moving toward the door, but Nancy's eyes were still on the couple. Olivia cradled Michael's head in one arm and was frantically waving the other at the innkeeper. Mrs. McVee was showing people out the door and didn't notice Olivia.

Nancy grabbed Ned's arm. "Something's wrong!" she hissed, pulling Ned with her toward Michael and Olivia.

"What happened?" Nancy asked as Ned eased Michael onto the carpet.

"I don't know." Olivia moaned. "But I think Michael's dead!"

Chapter

Two

Nancy put a hand on Michael's neck. "He's not dead," she announced after feeling a pulse. She leaned over him and felt his shallow breath on her face.

"He was supposed to keel over—he's written in as the first victim in the murder mystery. I thought he was just acting," Olivia said, visibly disturbed.

Mrs. McVee had shown the last guest out of the dining room and now approached the group surrounding Michael. "What's going on?" she asked.

"Call nine-one-one," Nancy told her. "Michael's really sick!"

"Right away," Mrs. McVee said.

"I'll go with you," Olivia said, and hurried out of the room with Mrs. McVee.

Ned knelt next to Michael on the floor. "He seemed fine earlier," he said.

Michael moaned. His eyes slowly opened, and he tried to sit up.

"Just stay still," Nancy told him. "We've called for help, and they'll be here any minute."

Ned grabbed a seat cushion and gently eased it under Michael's head. "You okay, buddy? You gave us a serious scare!" he said.

"Phew!" Michael said weakly. "I haven't felt this bad since I was a kid and home with a fever."

"Maybe that's what it is," Ned said to Nancy. "The flu." He leaned over Michael. "You'll be okay, buddy," Ned told him. "Just keep still until the ambulance arrives."

"Ambu—" Michael tried to say, but he couldn't finish. He put his hands over his stomach, wincing with pain.

Soon there were sirens, and moments later two emergency medical attendants quickly entered the room. They began checking Michael over.

Mrs. McVee led Nancy and Ned out of the room. "I'm sure he'll be fine," she said soothingly.

Nancy put her arm around Ned's waist. "I know it looks serious, but he probably just has the flu," she said. "Who knows what kind of weird bugs are floating around Emerson." Ned smiled.

The fraternity brothers and their dates were

now crowding the lobby, anxious for news. Mrs. McVee quietly told them about Michael and urged them to go into the parlor where coffee and dessert were being served. Mia came bounding down the stairs. "What's going on?" she asked. "I heard the sirens while I was waiting for Michael in my room."

Ned told her about Michael's collapse. "Oh, no!" Mia exclaimed. "I told him to take it easy," she said. "He was feeling tired this morning, and I was afraid he was coming down with something."

The attendants wheeled Michael out of the dining room on a gurney. Mia ran over to Michael and spoke softly to him. Ned, Nancy, and Mia followed the gurney outside to the ambulance. Mia climbed inside with Michael, and the ambulance sped off down the road. Ned walked back to the lobby.

"I'm sure Mia will let us know what's going on," Ned told Nancy.

Nancy nodded. "It's strange, though, that the illness hit him in the middle of the play."

"Yeah," Ned agreed. "But at least we were around to help him. What if this had happened when he was alone in his room?"

"You're right," Nancy answered. "Timing is everything."

"Do you want some coffee?" Ned asked. "I could really use a cup."

Something caught Nancy's attention at the

front desk. "Sure. I'll meet you in the parlor in a couple of minutes."

Nancy walked past the desk, where she had noticed that Mrs. McVee and a husky, red-haired guy were speaking in hushed tones. Nancy stopped in the hallway and leaned out of sight against the wall, hoping to overhear what was being said.

"Are you sure you checked the kitchen thoroughly?" Nancy heard Mrs. McVee ask.

"I'm sure," came the gruff reply.

"I don't know what made that boy sick," Mrs. McVee said, "but I don't want anyone thinking it was food poisoning!"

"Everything was fine," the guy answered. "No one else is sick, so I think we're okay."

Just then several people emerged from the library. Nancy hurriedly made her way to the parlor, where she found Ned sitting with some of his friends.

"We were just talking about Michael," Ned told her, pulling out a chair next to him.

Nancy sat down and poured herself a cup of coffee from the pot on the table. She added milk and took a sip. "I hope nobody else comes down with this bug," she said.

"That's what we were thinking," Paul Jensen, a senior, said. "I can't imagine being sick even for a day with the workload I've got this semester."

"Yeah," said a girl Nancy didn't know. "If

Michael is out for long, he might not be able to catch up."

Nancy stared into her cup. Something was bothering her about the timing of Michael's illness. It fit too well into the scene of the play. If Michael had been feeling sick earlier, why hadn't he said something?

"Nan?" Ned asked. "Are you okay?"

Nancy snapped out of her musing. "Yes," she said. "I was just thinking."

"Well, I was just thinking that I'd better go square things away with Mrs. McVee," Ned said, running a hand through his dark hair. "With Number One in the hospital, I'd better keep an eye on the logistics of the weekend." He stood up and stretched. "Will you excuse me?"

"Sure," Nancy answered. "I'm going to sit here and finish my coffee. I'll catch you later."

Ned leaned over and gave Nancy a kiss. "Okay, then," he said.

Conversation hummed around Nancy as she sat, sipping her coffee and thinking. She didn't believe in coincidences. Michael's getting sick at just the right time in the play was too much of a coincidence. She had an idea. She set down her coffee cup and stood. "I'll see you guys in the morning," she said to the group.

Once she was out in the hallway she headed for the dining room. It looked just as it had when they wheeled Michael out. Apparently in all the excitement, no one had cleaned up the props from the play. Nancy walked over to the table and gingerly picked up Michael's cup. In the light of the lamp, she noticed something floating in the remains of the tea at the bottom of the cup.

"That's strange," she said. She picked up the cup and swirled the leftover tea around. There was a thin, oily film floating on top. She put the cup down and examined Olivia's leftover tea. It looked fine. The tea in the pot also seemed normal, but when she picked up a small pitcher and held it in the light, she saw the same oily film on top of the milk. Nancy remembered that Michael had taken milk in his tea, but Olivia didn't. Maybe he *was* poisoned!

Nancy heard the noise of clinking dishes and hastily hid the teacup on the floor behind a heavy drapery.

She had just stood up when she heard a deep voice demanding, "What are you doing?"

Startled, Nancy looked up and saw the red-headed guy who had been talking to Mrs. McVee.

"I repeat, what are you doing here?" he asked.

"I was just putting the teacups back on the tray," she answered, reaching for Olivia's cup, then putting it on the tray next to several unused cups.

"In case you didn't know," he snapped, "that's my job."

Nancy stared at him, surprised by his hostility. She placed the milk pitcher back on the tray.

"You are the guest," he said sarcastically, "and

I am the help. Now, go be the guest!" He motioned to the door for Nancy to leave.

"Sorry," Nancy said, irritated. What was with this guy anyway? She didn't want the milk pitcher cleaned if there was poison in it, but she couldn't see a way to get around this guy—especially when she was only going on a gut instinct that Michael had been poisoned. She was glad she had hidden the teacup. She left the room as the guy started to clear the table.

In the lobby she saw Mrs. McVee at the front desk, talking with Ned.

"I was just in the dining room with a very interesting guy," Nancy said to the innkeeper. "The one with the red hair? He was picking up the tea service from the play."

"Oh, that's Jim," Mrs. McVee told her. "Jim Haines. He handles the props for our murder mystery weekends. He's responsible for so many things around the inn, I'm surprised he's never slipped up and put the wrong props together for a scene."

"It sounds like he's got a big job here," Nancy said.

"He's invaluable to me," Mrs. McVee said. "He works here to help pay for his tuition at Emerson College."

"He goes to Emerson?" Nancy asked, surprised.

"Yes," Mrs. McVee said, "and he works here every weekend. Whenever there's a special event, like this weekend, it seems as if he ends up doing just about everything to make things run smoothly."

Ned and Mrs. McVee finished talking, then she excused herself.

"Do you know this guy Jim?" Nancy asked Ned.

"Yeah, vaguely. He rushed our fraternity but didn't get in. He's got a big chip on his shoulder, and nobody could stand him."

Nancy could see why the Omega Chi brothers had turned Jim Haines down. With his attitude, who would want to hang out with him? It was good that he worked behind the scenes at the inn, she thought, because he sure didn't know how to deal with the guests in person.

"Hey. Alone at last with the lovely Nancy Drew, to borrow a line from Derek Waverly," Ned said. "Want to sit by the fire in the front parlor for a few minutes?"

"Sounds good," Nancy said. Ned wasn't the only one with that idea, Nancy thought. There were several other couples sitting on couches and chairs near the fire.

They sat down on a cozy loveseat, and Ned wrapped his arms around Nancy. "This is great. I'm so happy we have some time to be together, Nan," Ned said, kissing her lightly, first on one cheek, then the other, then on her mouth. Nancy kissed back, but was obviously distracted.

"Nan? Hello?"

"I'm sorry, Ned," Nancy began, "I just can't help thinking Michael's illness is a little too coincidental." Ned groaned. "No, really, Ned. I mean the play calls for Michael to be the first victim, and then he falls over for real, and he's seriously sick? It's too much!"

"Don't tell me this has morphed from a romantic weekend into another of your investigations," Ned said.

"Ned, listen to me. I found a suspicious film in Michael's teacup and none in Olivia's. I'm telling you I'm not at all convinced it's just the flu Michael's been hit with."

"I think you're off base this time, Nancy. You're taking this murder mystery thing way too seriously! It's just for fun, it's all staged, and Michael has a bug that hit him hard because he's been working too much. That's all. Okay?"

"Okay," Nancy said, although she still didn't buy it.

Ned yawned, then looked at his watch. "It's getting late, and there's a lot happening tomorrow. We'd better get some sleep. Want me to walk you to your room?" He stood up.

"No, thanks, Ned. You go on. I'll head up in a minute."

"Okay, then," said Ned. He took Nancy's face in his hand and tenderly stroked her cheek. "I love you, Nan," he said.

"I love you, too," she said. They arranged to

meet at eight the next morning, then Nancy kissed Ned good night.

As she watched him walk into the lobby she thought about how good his arms felt around her. She smiled again.

A few minutes later Nancy heard the front door open. From the parlor, she could see Mia crossing the lobby. She looked tired, Nancy thought.

"Mia," Nancy called, "how's Michael?"

"Oh, hi, Nancy. He's a little better," Mia said, coming into the now-deserted parlor. "The doctors aren't sure what's wrong with him."

"It's not the flu?" Nancy inquired.

"Not as far as they can tell," Mia said, sitting down on the couch with Nancy.

"Have they tested for anything else?" Nancy asked. "Like poison?"

"Poison?" Mia responded, looking shocked.

"You know, food poisoning or something," Nancy said. "Maybe it was something he ate earlier in the day."

Mia relaxed a bit and ran a hand through her long blond hair. "Not that I know of. We ate at a diner for lunch, but we've eaten there a lot of times. The doctors haven't said anything like that, but I know they'll be watching him closely," she said.

"Ned and I will check on him tomorrow," Nancy said, getting up from the loveseat.

"You won't be able to stay long," Mia warned. "Michael's pretty out of it, and the doctors want him to rest."

"That's fine," Nancy said. "Well, I'm ready for bed. You must be beat, too."

"Yeah, I'll walk up with you," said Mia. They went up the stairs to their rooms. "Why don't you knock on my door tomorrow, say around ten?" Mia asked as she stopped at her door. "We can go to the hospital together."

"Sounds good to me," Nancy said. "It looks like there are a couple of murder mystery segments in the morning; we can zip over there between them. I'll let Ned know at breakfast."

"Great!" Mia said. "Good night, Nancy."

" 'Night, Mia," Nancy said as she opened her own door.

Nancy looked at the clock beside her bed and realized it was even later than she'd thought. She changed into her nightgown, washed up, then climbed into bed. Ah, she thought. Sleep!

Nancy's body was tired, but her mind wouldn't stop racing. After more than an hour of tossing and turning, she got out of bed, pulled on her robe, and quietly let herself out of her room. Although well lit, the halls were empty now, and the inn had the feel of deep night. Nancy crept down the stairs and into the dining room. She crossed the room and pushed through the double doors into the now dark kitchen. Where would that tea set be? she wondered. Her musing was interrupted by a whoosh of air behind her.

She turned around quickly. "Who's there?" she asked. There was no response. In the darkness, all she could see was a tall, dark figure stepping out of the shadows and moving toward her, quickly and silently.

Chapter

Three

Nancy held her breath. She knew she was plainly visible in the weak shaft of moonlight coming in through the kitchen window.

The figure stopped. There was a long moment of silence followed by "You again! What are you doing in here?"

Nancy recognized Jim Haines's voice. She backed away a few steps, but her retreat was blocked by a kitchen counter. She felt what she thought must be the tea set on the counter behind her.

"I'm just looking around," Nancy said.

Jim snorted. "In the middle of the night? Why so secretive? Who are you, anyway?"

"I'm Nancy Drew," she said. "Pleased to meet you," she added breezily, trying to mask the unease she felt.

"Well, I'm certainly not pleased to meet you," was his brusque reply.

"Look, I just wanted to check out that tea set, and I didn't have a chance earlier, that's all. Did you put the tray together for the play?"

"As always," he answered. "Why do you want to know?"

Nancy felt around and flicked on a light under the shelf above the counter. She saw the milk pitcher there. Clean, she thought. So much for that piece of evidence.

"I was curious," she said. "My friend Michael was the one taken to the hospital, and I wanted to make sure nothing he ate or drank at the inn made him sick."

"What?" Jim bellowed. "Nothing here made that guy sick! I heard he has the flu."

"That may be," Nancy said, "but I heard Mrs. McVee talking about checking the kitchen, and I was just wondering."

"So," he said, glaring at her, "you're snooping around, trying to make trouble!" He took a step toward her, his hands balled into fists at his sides. "Stay out of it. One member of your frat party's in the hospital," he hissed, "and we'd hate to make it two!"

"I get your meaning," Nancy said, undaunted. "We'd also hate to think that you had anything to do with it, wouldn't we?"

"How dare you accuse me?" he shouted. "I've

had enough of your questions. How about I show you out?"

"Never mind," Nancy said. "I'm leaving." She turned and went back through the double doors into the darkened dining room. She stopped and listened for a second and heard Jim banging dishes around. Quickly she ran to the curtain where she'd hidden the teacup earlier, picked it up, and carefully carried it upstairs to her room. Then she locked the door behind her.

Nancy hid the teacup under her bed, hung up her robe, then crawled into bed. It took a few minutes for her heartbeat to slow down, but at last she fell asleep.

Nancy woke Saturday morning to a beautiful, sunny day. She opened the window, letting in fresh air. The curtains billowed in the breeze, and Nancy took a deep breath. She laid out her jeans and a cream-colored sweater, then headed for the bathroom. When she was ready, she went downstairs to meet Ned. She expected to find him waiting for her, but he wasn't in the lobby.

"Hey, Nancy!" called Matt, who was standing beside a tray of coffee and juice set out for early risers. "Can I pour you some coffee?" he asked.

"Morning, Matt! Thanks, but I'll wait for Ned. Have you seen him, by any chance?" she asked.

"Yeah, I saw him go outside a few minutes ago. Actually, my date's missing, too. I hope she wasn't the next victim!"

Nancy laughed. "I hope not. Good luck finding her." She went out onto the front porch and looked around. She spotted Ned sitting on a bench—with a cute blond girl huddled beside him.

Ned and the girl were so absorbed in their conversation, neither one saw Nancy approach.

"Good morning, Ned," Nancy said. The two quickly separated and stood up.

"Nancy," Ned said, "this is Trish Mays."

"Nice to meet you," Nancy said, extending her hand.

Trish shook Nancy's hand, visibly uncomfortable. "I think I should get going, Ned," Trish stammered. "Thanks for the help." She hurried away to leave Ned and Nancy alone.

"So, what kind of help was Dr. Nickerson dispensing today?" Nancy asked.

"Nothing much. Just letting Trish in on what's up with Michael," Ned told her.

"She seemed kind of tense," Nancy said.

"Yeah," Ned answered. "She cornered me when I got downstairs and herded me out here for a private talk."

Ned told Nancy about Trish as they walked inside. "It's a little complicated," he said. "Trish is Michael's ex-girlfriend. After he broke up with her, she kept calling him and following him around campus. When Michael started seeing Mia, Trish's behavior got even worse. The word is, she called him so many times that he finally changed his phone number. Then Trish started going out with Matt," Ned continued. "Matt is a really good guy, and I'm afraid Trish used him to get an invitation to this weekend."

"Okay, but why did she want to talk privately to you?" Nancy asked.

"She didn't want anyone else to know she was interested in Michael's condition," Ned replied. "So she asked me. She knows I'll keep quiet."

"Well, I'll say one thing for you, Nickerson. You are a man of integrity!" Nancy said as Ned blushed. "But seriously, do you think I could talk to Trish about last night? If she's watching Michael so carefully, maybe she noticed something someone else didn't."

"Sure, but you should watch *her* carefully," Ned said. "Trish isn't exactly stable these days."

"Speaking of unstable . . ." Nancy quickly related her encounter with Jim Haines the night before.

"Just be careful, Nancy, okay?" he said as they went in for breakfast.

In the dining room, they were amused to see the "guests" from the play milling about, totally in character. Mrs. Wendham was flitting about, asking the people at each table if they were enjoying their stay.

Mrs. McVee stepped into the dining room and tapped a knife on a glass to get everyone's attention. "Just a brief announcement, everyone," she began. "Despite the events of last night, with one of our guests falling ill at a moment coincidental with the plot of our mystery, the show will naturally go on as planned. I'm sure you're all aware by now that your fraternity president is resting comfortably at the hospital—a forced break from a strenuous college schedule is apparently just what he needed," she said. "Well, enjoy the weekend!"

A moment later, Mrs. Wendham stopped at Ned and Nancy's table.

"Having a good time?" she asked.

"Absolutely!" Ned answered.

"Mrs. Wendham," said Nancy, "do you mind if I ask you a few questions?"

"Not at all, dear," the actor said, remaining in character.

"Any idea who might have had access to the tea tray last night before or during the dinner scene?"

"Well, let's see . . . myself and Olivia, Derek, Robert, Mickey, and of course, Jeffrey. Also that helpful young man about the inn, Jim Haines, I believe his name is. Any of the other guests might've wandered into the kitchen—oh, I do

33

recall seeing a blond-haired girl in there before dinner, not one of the kitchen workers. Is that helpful?"

"Yes, thank you, Mrs. Wendham," Nancy said, smiling.

"Good, then. Glad you're having fun!" She moved on.

Ned set down his coffee cup and studied Nancy's face. "Your line of questioning doesn't have much to do with the murder mystery weekend," he said. "I can see your detective powers are otherwise occupied, which gives *me* all the more chance of winning!"

"You're really getting into this, aren't you?" Nancy said.

"It's fun!" he said, watching Mrs. Wendham leave the dining room. "Too bad you still think there's a real mystery to solve, or we could be having fun together."

Derek Waverly began speaking loudly just then, indicating the start of another segment of the murder mystery.

"Lighten up, Olivia," he said, pouring himself a cup of coffee from the urn on the sideboard. "It's not the end of the world!"

"How could you be so insensitive?" Olivia demanded, glaring at him. "My fiancé is dead!" She was sitting at a table for two, and she looked as though she'd been crying.

"No great loss," Derek said coldly. "You can do better, Olivia."

34

"I've told you plainly that I'm not interested in you, Derek. Besides, as I also told you, Michael had information that will lead to the recovery of Mother's diamonds."

Derek Waverly looked sharply at Olivia and then leaned casually against the sideboard. "And did he impart this information before his untimely death?"

"As a matter of fact, yes." She pulled a crumpled piece of paper out of a small purse. "He gave me this clipping last night before he collapsed. It's an obituary of a woman named Roseann Harriman Long. Poor Michael died before he could tell me what it means," Olivia said, fighting back tears, "but I'll find out."

Just then Robert Jones walked into the dining room. When Derek saw Robert approaching, he quickly set his coffee cup down and hurried to the table. The two men fairly ran to grab the chair beside Olivia. Robert won, sitting down clumsily, and shot Derek a triumphant look as Olivia dried her eyes and slipped the clipping back into her purse.

"What is this, musical chairs?" she asked.

"This room has just gotten much too crowded," said Derek. "Time for me to be going. I'll be seeing *you* later," he added, speaking directly to Olivia.

After Derek had left, Robert Jones pushed his eyeglasses up on his nose and wiped the palms of his hands on his thighs before reaching for Olivia's hand. "Olivia, you know I'm desperately in love with you!" The guests laughed at Olivia's horrified expression. She pulled her hand away from his.

"I'm glad Michael's out of the picture, Olivia. You deserve a man with a bright future—like me. I'm smarter than I look. And I get what I want."

Jeffrey accompanied Mrs. Wendham into the dining room then, followed by Derek Waverly, Mickey Sloan, and a tall, slim man wearing a trenchcoat and hat. They walked over to Olivia's table.

Mrs. Wendham introduced the newcomer. "This is Detective Ryan," she said. The detective flashed a badge around the table. "He has something to say about Michael's death, although I can't imagine what. I believe we answered all relevant questions for the police last night." She motioned toward Jeffrey and the tea service on the sideboard. "Would you like some tea, Detective?"

"No, thank you," Detective Ryan said, pushing his hat back on his head. "The tea around here seems to contain more than just tea leaves!"

"I can understand your reluctance to see me, Mrs. Wendham, since"—the detective stopped and stared at her—"you are all suspects!"

There was a commotion as everyone hastened to proclaim his or her innocence.

"Please sit down," Detective Ryan said. "I think you need to hear what I have to say." The group slowly took seats, except for Jeffrey, who was still on duty and remained standing by the tea service.

"It seems that our questions from last night have produced an unexpected result," the detective continued. "We have determined that you all had the opportunity to poison the tea."

"I—I thought we explained everything last night," Jeffrey stammered.

"Surely, there is the question of motive," Mickey piped up, tossing a mane of red hair that had been concealed by her hat the previous night. "What could I possibly have against Michael?"

"That is what I intend to find out, Ms. Sloan," Detective Ryan answered. "We believe that the murder has something to do with Mrs. Wendham's stolen diamonds, and I think we'll be able to make the connection to one of you in no time!"

"Awfully sure of yourself, aren't you, Detective?" asked Derek. "You people haven't found the diamonds, so what makes you think you can find a killer?"

The detective ignored the insult. "We are on top of this case, Mr. Waverly," Ryan answered.

"I must insist that all of you remain at the inn until the investigation has been completed. Thank you for your time." Detective Ryan tipped his hat to them and left.

They were all silent for a moment. Both Olivia and Jeffrey appeared drained, while the others started clamoring at once.

"Of all the nerve," Mrs. Wendham said. "How dare he suspect me!"

"I think Detective Ryan is trying to make us suspect one another," Mickey pointed out.

"I don't have anything to hide!" Derek proclaimed.

"I barely knew the man," Robert said, shifting his legs uneasily.

"He was my fiancé!" Olivia whimpered. "How could they think I would hurt him?"

"Enough of this!" Mrs. Wendham demanded. "We have to stay put until the police stop this nonsense, so let's make the best of it. Pass the croissants, please."

The actors began eating, and the scene was over.

"So who do you think is the prime suspect?" Nancy asked Ned as they finished eating their muffins.

"I'm not sure," Ned said. "I don't know what to make of the obituary as a lead on the diamond heist. We're going to need more information about that. Meanwhile, we know Derek and

Robert are both in love with Olivia, giving each of them motives for wanting Michael out of the picture."

"Yes, Robert seems a competitive kind of guy," Nancy mused. Much like Mia, she thought.

"What do you say we go for a walk?" Nancy said, changing the subject.

Nancy and Ned strolled along the gravel drive that led to the main road, enjoying the fall colors and talking. On the way back, Nancy told Ned about her plan to take Michael's teacup to the hospital, to have the contents tested.

"Nan," Ned said, "don't you think you're getting a little carried away?"

"No, I don't," Nancy said. "I don't believe his getting sick immediately after drinking the tea is a coincidence. Besides," Nancy went on, "maybe it's some kind of poisoning, and the best way to determine that is to test the tea. So either way—"

"Nancy is on the job again," Ned teased. More seriously he added, "If it'll help them find out what's wrong with Michael, I'm all for it."

As they approached the inn Nancy saw Olivia sitting in a lounge chair by the pool. "I'd like to go over and ask Olivia a question," Nancy said.

Ned raised an eyebrow. "Trying to get some inside information about who did it?"

"No," Nancy said with a laugh. "I think I have

the skills to win on my own. I want to see if she has any information about what might have happened to Michael last night." She grabbed Ned's arm. "Come with me."

Nancy introduced herself and Ned to Olivia and told her how much everyone was enjoying the play.

"Glad to hear it," Olivia said, smiling. "We all feel terrible that Michael's sick and can't see the fallout from his 'death.'"

"Me, too," said Nancy. "Listen, can you tell me who knew ahead of time that Michael was going to be the first victim?"

"Sure, everybody knew. At least everybody in the company, as well as Mrs. McVee and that Jim Haines guy. What a charmer."

"I know what you mean," Nancy said wryly. She thanked Olivia, then she and Ned headed inside.

"I'll run upstairs and get Mia," Nancy said to Ned. "She told me to knock on her door when we were ready to leave for the hospital."

"Okay. Meanwhile, I'll call the hospital to make sure that Michael can have visitors," Ned said.

Upstairs, Nancy knocked on Mia's door several times but got no answer. Cautiously she turned the knob and found the door unlocked. Slowly she opened it and peered inside.

She didn't see Mia, and Nancy had a terrible feeling that something was wrong. She walked in and saw the phone off the hook and dangling on the far side of the bed. Books and papers littered the floor.

As Nancy walked around the bed to hang up the phone she heard a low groan. There, sprawled on the floor, was Mia.

Chapter

Four

"Mia!" Nancy cried. Mia strugged to get up, and Nancy crouched beside her to help.

"What happened?" Mia asked slowly.

"I was hoping you could tell me that," Nancy said. "Hold on, let me get you a glass of water." Nancy stepped into the bathroom and filled a water glass for Mia. When she came back, Mia was sitting in one of the chairs by the window.

"Are you all right?" Nancy asked.

"I think I'm fine," Mia replied, and took the water. "Give me a minute and I'll tell you for sure."

Nancy picked up papers and books from the floor and replaced the receiver on the phone. "Did you hit your head or something?" she asked. "Would you like me to call a doctor?"

"No, no doctor," Mia said anxiously. "I just

sort of fainted. It was the phone. . . ." she said in a whisper.

"What about the phone?" Nancy asked, puzzled.

"I got this awful phone call." Mia's voice was so low that Nancy could barely hear her.

Mia looked close to tears, so Nancy asked quietly, "What did they say?"

Mia hesitated a moment. "They said that what happened to Michael was no accident," she answered in a shaky voice. "They said that if I wasn't careful, I'd be next!" She put her head in her hands.

"Mia, you have to tell me everything," Nancy said gently. "Why would someone want to hurt Michael, and now you?" Nancy stopped to let Mia compose herself.

"I don't know, Nancy," Mia said, sipping the water. "I just don't know!"

Something about the phone call triggered a connection in Nancy's mind. Ned had said that Trish Mays used to call and harass Michael. Maybe she was bothering Mia now.

"I'm going down to the lobby to get Ned," Nancy told her. "I'll send him up here to be with you while I check something out." She left Mia sitting there and hurried downstairs.

She found Ned sitting in one of the overstuffed chairs in the front parlor, reading the newspaper. He saw her urgent expression and got up. "Someone called Mia and threatened her," Nancy said quickly. "She's pretty shaken."

"Who was it?" Ned asked.

"I don't know," Nancy answered, "but now I know I was on the right track about Michael being poisoned."

Ned looked alarmed. "What do you mean?"

"The caller told Mia that what happened to Michael was no accident!" she said. "Can you go up and stay with her for a couple of minutes? I need to check on something. See if you can get her to describe any of the details of the phone call."

Ned looked concerned. "Sure, whatever you need, Nancy."

"Thanks," she said.

Ned started upstairs, while Nancy looked around for the inn's operator. She found her in a room beside the lobby. Nancy knocked lightly on the open door. "Excuse me, could I ask you a question?" she asked.

"What can I help you with?" the gray-haired woman asked.

"There was a phone call to Room Twenty-two about ten or fifteen minutes ago," Nancy told her. "Can you tell me if the call came from an outside line or from another room here?"

"I didn't put any calls through to that room," the operator answered. "I've mostly been sending calls through to the office."

"How about the calls from room to room?" Nancy asked.

"I can't tell you about those," the operator said. "This system doesn't monitor those calls. Someone can call a room from any phone in the inn, and I won't see it. I only get the outside calls and dispatch them." The phone rang, and the operator turned to answer it.

Nancy tapped her on the shoulder and mouthed a thank-you, then left the room. She knew there were phones in each of the guest rooms, plus phones in each of the common and administration rooms. She had seen two in the dining room alone. That meant the call hadn't necessarily come from a guest or staff member— someone could just as easily have walked into the inn from outside and placed a call from one of the public rooms. It would be nearly impossible to trace the call.

Nancy went up to Mia's room and found Ned out in the hall, leaning against Mia's door. "Guarding the door now, are we?" she said, grinning. "How is she?"

"Better than when I got here. She's just cleaning up, and—oh! I didn't get a chance to tell you. Visiting hours don't start till noon, so I suggested to Mia that we could all do something together this morning."

"Sure," Nancy said, her tone distant.

"Nan, are you okay?" Ned asked.

"Fine, but my big idea turned into a big nothing," she told him. "I was hoping to find out where the call came from, but all I discovered was that it was placed from inside the inn."

"Knowing you, I'm sure you'll find out who it was." He gave her a cheerful smile.

Nancy didn't feel so confident. "Did Mia tell you anything about the caller?" she asked.

"She couldn't tell if it was male or female," he said. "She told me the voice was muffled." Just then the door opened, and Mia came out.

"Listen, I don't think I'm up to doing anything right now," Mia said. Nancy noted that Mia had freshened her makeup, though, and was now wearing her blond hair pulled back into a high ponytail.

"Oh, that's okay," Ned replied. "I'm sure you need a little time to recover."

"Yeah, I feel a little shaky still, and I really should hit the books again anyhow. I have a huge exam on Tuesday. Thanks a lot for taking care of me, both of you. I really appreciate it." Mia smiled, then shut the door.

As they started down the hall, Ned said, "She's looking a lot better."

"Yes, she is," Nancy agreed as they went downstairs.

"Since we're not going to the hospital till this afternoon, do you want to go out by the lake and lose to me at archery?" Nancy asked with a wicked grin.

"A challenge? You're on," Ned said.

They raced down to the archery targets and found Matt there practicing by himself.

"Hey, buddy," Ned called. "What are you doing all alone on a potentially romantic weekend?"

"Trish was supposed to meet me here, but I guess she's standing me up again," Matt said.

"Her loss," said Ned. "Yours, too, if you play me," he teased as he grabbed a bow and arrow. "Drew here has already volunteered to be slaughtered. I'll gladly murder you, too, Matt."

"A boy can dream, Nickerson." Nancy laughed.

Ned shot his first arrow wide of the mark. "Better luck next time," Nancy said. Her first arrow went *zing!* toward the bull's-eye.

Ned and Matt tried their best, but before long it was clear that Nancy was by far the superior marksperson.

"Okay, I give up," Ned said with a mock growl. "But this contest isn't over yet, Drew. You just wait till the next round."

"Surrender accepted," Nancy said, laughing. She went over and put her arm through his. "In the meantime, let's say we put down our bows and check out the next part of the mystery. I see the actors over there, and they look about ready to start."

Matt spied Trish among the guests gathered at the edge of the lake and went to stand beside her.

Nancy looked around and saw a few of the hotel staff, but was glad Jim didn't seem to be with them.

Everyone quieted down as Derek Waverly appeared along the shore. He looked all around, checking behind bushes and trees, until he appeared to be satisfied he was alone. Then he went to the lake and waited.

Mickey Sloan came out of the trees, picking leaves and twigs from her hair. The two of them started speaking loudly, seemingly unaware they were being overheard.

"What is this all about?" Mickey asked. "Why did you want to meet me out here?"

"You know the answer to that!" Derek hissed. "After all, you're the one blackmailing me!"

"Blackmailing you?" she repeated, raising her pencil-thin eyebrows. "Why would I do that?"

Derek sneered. "According to your clever little note, you know something about me that the police would like to know." He took a step closer to her.

"I know quite a lot about you, Waverly," she said coolly, "and none of it is good. After all, getting information is my business!"

"So what about the note?" he asked her. "Something to connect me with the diamonds, you wrote. What do you want?"

Mickey was busy brushing herself off, not in a hurry to answer him. Derek paced around, growing more agitated, until he finally shouted, "I demand that you tell me what you know! And what you want for keeping your information from the police."

"What I want," she told him, "is for you to leave me alone. I didn't write any note, and I'm not interested in any of your criminal doings." She tossed her red hair and looked Derek up and down. "Oh, I *could* blackmail you," she said. "I know all about the gambling debts you've run up with Wendham company money—but that doesn't have anything to do with me. I know what's fair, and I only want what's rightfully mine. You might be an embezzler, but I'm not your blackmailer."

"I don't believe you, and actually, I have some information of my own about you, Ms. Sloan. If that is your real name!" Derek said, raising his voice still further.

As Derek continued to badger Mickey, Nancy was distracted from the staged argument by a real argument going on behind her. She turned around to see Trish and Matt having a heated discussion.

Nancy maneuvered her way around the edge of the crowd until she was just a few feet behind Trish and Matt.

"I told you that I want to break up!" Trish was saying to Matt. "Michael needs me more than ever now."

Matt's face was red with anger. "So what were you doing, using me so you could keep an eye on Michael?"

"Was it so wrong to want to be around Michael?" Trish asked. "You've always known how I felt about him."

"It was wrong of you to use me like that!" Matt shot back, obviously hurt. "Oh, and in case you forgot, Michael doesn't need you. He has a girlfriend!" Matt stormed off.

Nancy watched as Trish stared after Matt. She was about to sneak back to her place next to Ned when she heard Trish say, "Not for long!" Trish took off down the path.

Nancy wound her way back to Ned. "Where'd you go?" he asked.

"I'll tell you later," Nancy said.

The argument between Derek and Mickey was just ending. "What'd I miss?" Nancy asked as the crowd broke up.

"Something tells me I should be asking what did *I* miss," Ned said.

Nancy laughed. "You first," she said.

Ned explained that Derek Waverly had alarmed Mickey by telling her he'd seen a certain obituary—Roseann Harriman Long's. The photo of the deceased showed a young woman wearing an exquisite diamond necklace. Mickey had had to struggle to regain her composure, and then she'd stormed off up the lawn.

"Your turn," prompted Ned.

Nancy related the argument between Matt and Trish. "You were right, Trish was using Matt to be near Michael," she said. "Also, she made some comment that was pretty disturbing—something about Mia not being Michael's girlfriend for long. She definitely had a motive for calling Mia, but I have to find a way to prove it."

"I feel bad for Matt," Ned said. "He doesn't deserve to be treated that way. I didn't think Trish would admit it to him."

"I think she did because she really believes that Michael needs her," Nancy said.

"Sounds crazy to me," Ned told her.

Nancy thought for a moment. "It does, but is it crazy enough for her to have poisoned Michael and threatened Mia?"

"But why would she poison Michael?" Ned asked.

"He broke up with her," Nancy explained. "Maybe it's a fatal attraction kind of thing."

"I just can't believe she'd go that far," Ned said.

Ned and Nancy followed the crowd wandering back up to the inn. Ned went to take care of some business in the office with Mrs. McVee, and Nancy decided to look for Trish. She found the blond girl sitting on a sofa in the parlor. Nancy sat down beside her.

"Can I talk to you for a minute?" she asked. Trish looked at her warily but nodded yes.

"I know you're worried about Michael. Ned

51

told me," she said. Trish looked alarmed, and Nancy continued. "Don't worry—I won't tell anyone. But I'd like you to help him if you can."

"How can I help Michael?" Trish asked. "He's in the hospital, and I'm here. Even if I went to visit him, I don't think he'd see me."

"It's about last night," Nancy explained. "I was wondering if you saw anything unusual during the murder mystery."

"I wasn't at dinner," Trish answered curtly. "I knew about Michael's little acting debut, and I wasn't interested in seeing it."

Nancy thought that was odd, but she decided not to press the issue. "I wouldn't have minded missing the part where Michael got carted off in an ambulance, myself," Nancy said. "But the rest of the action was really good. Did you see it this morning?"

"Yes, I did," Trish said, relaxing a bit. "I think the characters and the costumes are terrific."

"So do I," Nancy responded. "I wouldn't mind having the dress Olivia wore. The fabric was beautiful."

Trish was starting to get into the conversation. "It was," she said. "And what about Mickey Sloan's hat? I saw one just like it at a mall last week. It cost a fortune!"

"What about Jeffrey?" Nancy asked, grinning. "I wonder how much starch they had to put into his suit to make him look so stiff?" They laughed.

"Yeah, he's the perfect butler. My money's

going to be on him just 'cause the butler always does it," Trish said, still giggling. She glanced at her watch, then quickly stood up. "Oh, I have to get going," she said. "I'm meeting another girl outside to see if we can stir up a game of doubles tennis. Want to join us?"

"No, but thanks," Nancy said.

Trish gave Nancy a little wave as she left.

Something that Trish had said bothered Nancy, but she couldn't quite pinpoint it. Trish had become friendly when they started talking about the costumes. . . .

That was it! Mickey Sloan had been wearing the expensive hat only in the dinner scene the night before—the scene Trish said she hadn't watched!

Chapter

Five

NANCY SAT FLIPPING through a magazine in the parlor, thinking about Trish. Trish had lied about not being around during the dinner scene the night before, and Mrs. Wendham said she'd seen a blond girl in the kitchen. Trish could have slipped something into the milk. She'd know that Michael drank milk in his tea, but would she have risked letting Olivia drink poisoned milk, too? If murder had been the intent, the poison would have been doubly deadly. Nancy wished she knew how Michael was doing.

Nancy's musings were interrupted by a kiss from Ned, who'd come up behind her.

"A sneak attack, no fair!" Nancy exclaimed.

"I've been looking all over for you," Ned said, sitting down beside her.

"I haven't been hiding," she answered. "As a matter of fact, I just had a nice chat with Trish."

"Interesting?" he asked.

"Very," Nancy said. "She says she wasn't at the dinner scene last night, but she slipped up, so I know she was there. I just don't know why she's lying."

"Ah, the plot thickens!" Ned said playfully.

"Ned, this is serious!" Nancy reminded him.

"Sorry, I know it is," he apologized. "You just let me know what I can do to help you."

"Nothing for right now, but thanks." Nancy stared into space, considering what she should do next.

"Earth to Nancy," Ned said, waving his hand in front of her face.

Nancy caught Ned's hand as it went by her. "I'm here," she said. "Just thinking too hard." She pulled Ned's arm over his head and tickled him in the ribs.

"Hey, no fair!" Ned cried. They wrestled for a minute, and Ned finally got his arms around Nancy, pinning her to the back of the sofa. They shared a quick kiss, aware that other people in the parlor were watching.

"We're making a spectacle of ourselves," Nancy whispered into Ned's ear.

Ned whispered back, "So what?" He kissed her again, then let her go.

"It's just about lunchtime," she announced. "Let's get going."

They sat at a table with Matt as well as two other Omega Chi brothers and their dates. Nancy made small talk with Matt, who looked dejected. As they ate from the lunch buffet, another segment of the mystery play began.

Jeffrey entered from the kitchen door, carrying a tray of small sandwiches. He was busy setting up Mrs. Wendham's lunch table when she came sweeping into the room with Olivia in tow. Mrs. Wendham's dress was a flowing violet silk, covered with a dainty floral pattern. Olivia wore a black miniskirt with a matching sweater. Mrs. Wendham went up to Jeffrey and fussed over the position of the silverware.

"I wish you'd concentrate on your work!" she huffed at him. "It's not as if you have to wait on the entire room, just this one table!"

"I'm sorry," Jeffrey said, giving her a sideways glance. "I hadn't finished the placement yet." He turned back to his work, muttering, "Never forgets, never forgives . . ."

Mrs. Wendham turned her back to him and took a sandwich. Jeffrey stuck his tongue out at her. Then he was once again the proper butler, tending to his duties.

"Did you see that?" Ned whispered, laughing.

"Yeah," Nancy answered. "I guess he's not the perfect butler after all!"

"Shh, here comes someone," Ned whispered.

Derek Waverly and Robert Jones entered the

dining room together, and when they saw Olivia, the two men again raced each other across the room to help her with her chair. The other diners laughed appreciatively.

Mickey Sloan walked into the dining room shortly after that and started to sit at Nancy's table. Derek stood and motioned her over to join Mrs. Wendham's table.

"Sit with us, Mickey, where I can keep an eye on you," he said, pulling out a chair for her.

"How's your little article coming along, dear?" Mrs. Wendham asked Mickey.

"Don't condescend to *me*, Katherine Wendham," Mickey snapped. "I can stir up enough to ruin you with just the stroke of my pen."

Jeffrey muttered, "Considering all that Wendham family dirt, a stiff breeze could stir up enough to ruin her."

Nancy and Ned glanced at each other, taking note of Jeffrey's comment.

"People in this town take my column seriously, even if you don't," Mickey said, "and don't think I won't miss an opportunity."

Mrs. Wendham eyed her cautiously. "Opportunity for what?" she asked.

"To tell what really happened to what you call *your* diamonds!" With that, Mickey ran out of the dining room, leaving behind a flabbergasted Derek and Mrs. Wendham.

After the characters had finished their lunch,

they milled about the dining room to chat with the guests and give them a chance to ask questions about the mystery.

Nancy called Robert Jones over to their table. "Do you know a woman named Roseann Long?" she asked.

"Nope, never heard of a Roseann Long," Robert replied.

Nancy asked Jeffrey the same question. He answered yes, then hurried away.

"Hey, Olivia," called Ned, waving the actress over to their table. "Is your hair color natural?" he asked.

Olivia smiled. "It certainly is," she said, giving him a wink.

"And do you wear contact lenses?" he asked.

"Nope, these big green eyes are for real."

When Olivia walked away to speak to another table, Nancy gave Ned a questioning look.

"Hey, I'm not sharing my investigative process with you, Nan," he joked. "You're on your own."

Ned asked Mickey the same questions about her hair and eyes, and her response was that hers, too, were natural.

Nancy asked, "I didn't hear your reply to Derek Waverly's question earlier today. *Is* Sloan your real name?"

Mickey smiled and shook her head.

Ned looked at Nancy. "I'll store that information away, too, Nancy, but I know I'm way ahead of you on this."

The actors were leaving the dining room, so Ned suggested a post-lunch game of volleyball, and everyone started gathering to go out to the back lawn.

"There's something I want to do," Nancy said to Ned. "I'll meet you after the game."

With a wave he was off, and Nancy was alone at the table. She finished her soda, and took a look around the room.

Carrying a large tray, Jim Haines came out of the service door from the kitchen. Nancy watched as he headed for her table. Uh-oh, here comes trouble, she thought. He reached the table and started clearing away the dishes.

Nancy decided to try a new approach. "Good meal this afternoon," she commented.

"I wouldn't know," he replied shortly. "I haven't eaten yet. We're short of staff, and I have to bus tables before I can eat."

Nancy continued to make small talk. "So I guess you do pretty much everything around here," she said, hoping to learn where he might have been when Mia got the phone call.

"Yeah," he said with a short laugh. "I do it all so you fraternity people can enjoy your little weekend. It makes my heart flutter to see all of you having a good time. Especially that Michael guy," he continued. "Looks like he had a real good time!"

Jim left the table with Nancy staring after him. So much for the friendly approach, she thought.

She did get one bit of information, though. Jim was bitter toward the fraternity guys, probably because he wasn't accepted when he rushed. But was he angry enough to get revenge by poisoning Michael?

Nancy left the dining room with this question swirling in her mind. She still favored Trish as a suspect and wanted to talk with her some more. She looked out the windows at the volleyball game but didn't see Trish there, so she went to the registration desk, got Trish's room number, then went upstairs. She knocked a couple of times and tried the door, but it was locked.

After a quick trip to her own room, Nancy returned with her lock-picking kit. If she couldn't talk to Trish, maybe she could get a clue from searching her room.

The hallway was deserted, and in moments Nancy had picked the lock and was inside the room. She searched through the dresser drawers, but all she found were Trish's clothes and a few pieces of jewelry, including an Omega Chi fraternity pin. She wondered if it might be Michael's. She hoped poor Matt hadn't given her his pin.

Next Nancy searched the bathroom, the closet, Trish's suitcase, and even her makeup bag, but found nothing. Frustrated, she sat on the bed and thought about where else she might look.

She had thought for sure that there would be something to link Trish to the threats. As she was about to leave, Nancy spotted something under the dresser. She picked it up. Examining it, Nancy determined that it was part of a label, probably from a bottle. She looked closer and read the words printed on it: "If ingested, seek medical attention immediately!" She squinted to see the last word, smoothing the crumpled corner of the label. She gasped as she read it.

Poison.

Chapter

Six

I NEED TO FIND Ned!" Nancy exclaimed. She stuffed the label into her jeans pocket and quickly left the room.

She was heading toward a rear door when she passed the library and spotted Mia, sitting on a sofa, surrounded by books and papers.

"Mia!" she said, stopping in the doorway. "Have you seen Ned?"

Mia looked up from her work. "No, I haven't," she answered. "Sit down. You look like you need to relax. I thought I'd let you know that I ended up going to see Michael anyway, right when visiting hours started. I couldn't find you and Ned, and Mrs. McVee told me the local bus line runs right by the hospital."

This got Nancy's attention. She sat down in an overstuffed armchair and asked, "How is he?"

"Getting a little better," Mia answered. "But he's so sick the doctor doesn't know when he'll be released."

"Have the doctors found out anything?" Nancy asked.

"No," Mia told her. "They're doing a lot of tests, and it'll take time to get the results. It's probably just an unusually bad flu, like we've thought all along, but I guess they want to make sure it's not an *E. coli* infection, or botulism or something."

Just then Nancy saw Ned coming in from the volleyball game. He paused at the doorway. "Back at the books again, Mia?" he asked. "This must be some exam you're getting ready for."

"I'm afraid I have some catching up to do," Mia replied. "Since I started dating Michael, I haven't spent as much time as I should have studying. He doesn't have to work as hard as I do. Everything comes so easily to him." She let out a sigh and searched for something in one of the piles.

"By the way," Nancy said, "what do you know about Trish Mays?"

"Michael's old girlfriend?" Mia asked. "She used to bother him a lot, but he put a stop to it."

"How did he stop her?" Nancy inquired.

"He finally told her to leave us alone once and for all," Mia told her.

"Was she bothering you, too?"

Mia thought about that for a moment. "Only if

she saw us together," she began. "She'd tell Michael that I was no good for him and stuff like that." She put her papers down and leaned closer to Nancy. "She still glares at me all the time, and I'll tell you, if looks could kill . . ."

It wasn't a *look* that almost killed Michael, Nancy thought. If what Mia said was true, Trish didn't hide her jealousy.

"Could it have been Trish who threatened you on the phone?" Ned asked her.

"It could have been," Mia answered, "but I'm not sure. Like I said, the voice was muffled."

"Just keep alert and let us know if anything else happens," Ned told her.

As Nancy got up to leave, she knocked a pile of papers off the coffee table in front of her.

"Oh, don't bother with those," Mia told her. "I'll pick them up."

"It'll just take a minute," Nancy said. "I hope I didn't get them too much out of order." She picked up a few and saw that they were all neatly written class notes. She glanced at the tops of the pages and noticed something odd. All the pages had Michael's name at the top.

"Michael's notes look incredibly well organized," Nancy said, hoping Mia would explain why she had them.

"Yes, they are," Mia answered. "His notes are always better than mine, so I'm using them to study for next week's exam." She continued to gather them up. "After all, it looks like Michael won't need them." She quickly took the papers out of Nancy's hands.

"Sorry about the mess," Nancy said. "We'll see you later." She took Ned's arm and propelled him down the hall.

"I found something in Trish's room," Nancy said quietly. "Let's go out on the porch, and I'll show you." They hurried outside. Nancy pulled the label out of her pocket and showed it to Ned.

"What do we do about it?" Ned asked.

"Nothing for now," Nancy said. "I don't know what was in the bottle, and I'm not even sure it has anything to do with Michael anyway."

"Maybe it's from something the cleaning people use," Ned said.

"I know one way to find out," she said. "I'll ask Jim."

"What?" Ned exclaimed. "I thought you were going to stay away from him!"

"He knows as much about running this place as anybody," she said. "Even Mrs. McVee said so."

"Okay, but don't forget we're here to have fun." Ned gave her a mischievous look. "Come on, let's go out on the lake. You can question Jim Haines later, can't you?"

Nancy was torn. She wanted to work on the case, yet it wasn't often the two of them had an entire weekend together. She could spend an hour on the lake. "Okay," she said, smiling. "But let me take my one piece of evidence upstairs first." As she went up the stairs she called over her shoulder, "My turn to row!"

A few minutes later, as they strolled down the lawn toward the lake, Ned and Nancy saw some other couples had the same idea; just one boat was still tied to the dock. They untied it, climbed into it, and Nancy took the oars and began to row. The sun was warm on their backs, and gold and red autumn leaves ringed the lake. For the moment, anyway, Nancy was able to forget her worries and just enjoy Ned's company. She saw that his eyes were closed. The handsome face she loved so much looked happy and serene. She felt happy, too.

Ned opened his eyes, as if sensing Nancy was studying him. He smiled. "This is the life," he said, sighing.

"Aren't you supposed to be reciting poetry while I row?" Nancy teased him.

"Hmm. Okay, here's one. Roses are red, violets are blue, I like it when you row, and I get to lie here like a slug."

Nancy rolled her eyes. "That doesn't even rhyme, Nickerson."

After a while Ned took a turn at the oars, and Nancy settled into a comfortable position.

"Roses are red—" Nancy began.

"Oh, no," groaned Ned.

"Roses are red, violets are blue, everything's magic when I'm with you," she finished.

Ned smiled and blushed. An hour later they were back at the dock. "That was great," Ned said as they tied up the boat.

"Yes, it was," Nancy said, linking her arm with Ned's as they walked along the dock toward the lawn.

Nancy gave a sigh of happiness and looked around at the beautiful surroundings. She pointed out Olivia, walking alone on the lawn.

"And look, the lovesick Robert Jones is tailing her," Nancy said, laughing.

"Yeah, and there's the equally lovesick Derek Waverly, trailing behind him," observed Ned.

They stopped and watched the actors making their way down the lawn toward a picturesque gazebo perched along the lakeshore. The three characters maintained the space between them as they walked, each seemingly unaware of being followed or observed.

"I don't remember seeing this on the schedule of mystery vignettes," said Ned.

"I think I saw it," said Nancy. "'A Brief Interlude,' it was called."

Olivia had walked through the gazebo and down the three steps on the other side and was continuing along the lake. Robert followed, a bit more closely now, and he, too, walked through the pretty structure. Lastly, Derek stepped into the gazebo and paused there a moment, watching Olivia and Robert. He leaned against the railing and crossed his arms over his chest.

Suddenly he tumbled over the railing and into the lake!

"Help!" he shouted as he wildly churned the water. "I can't swim!"

Instinctively, Nancy sprinted over to the gazebo and dived headfirst into the lake.

Chapter

Seven

THERE WAS A DROP-OFF by the gazebo, and the water was unexpectedly deep. Derek Waverly was flailing his arms so wildly that Nancy had difficulty pulling the actor in toward shore.

"I've got you," she said, gasping. "Just try to calm down."

Ned and some of the other guys helped Nancy and Derek out of the water. They lay the actor out on the lawn and knelt beside him.

Derek gasped and coughed, and then, surprisingly, his splutters turned into laughter.

Nancy sat back on her heels and crossed her arms across her chest to try and get warm. "What's so funny?" she asked.

The actor lay there laughing a moment more, then sat up and leaned toward Nancy. He grinned.

"Are you okay?" Nancy asked a little nervously.

"Oh, outstanding, outstanding. Especially considering I was supposed to die a horrible death in that scene!"

There was a moment's silence, and then everybody broke out laughing.

"Hey, the guests are supposed to be participants, right?" said Ned. "How were we supposed to know?"

"Well, thanks for saving me, but for the sake of the plot, let's just consider me drowned and dead, okay? Now why don't you all heave to and carry me inside. Corpse that I am, I can't very well walk there myself." He winked and closed his eyes.

Ned and three of his fraternity brothers labored to pick Derek up, then started carrying him up the lawn.

"Oh," said Derek, snapping his eyes open, "someone might want to check the gazebo for clues. Just a little hint from Beyond!" He gave a ghostly wail and shut his eyes for good.

"I'll check," Nancy said.

"You'd better share the information, Drew," Ned said.

Nancy laughed and ran over to the gazebo. She found that the railing had been sawed through. Then she ran to tell Ned. He and the other guys had just put Derek on the porch.

"Okay, now we're really getting somewhere," he said.

"Okay, now we're really getting cold," said Nancy, wringing out her hair. "I'm going up to dry off and change my clothes."

Nancy bounded inside and up the stairs, hoping she wasn't leaving wet footprints behind her. In her room, she got out of her wet clothes, took a hot shower, then dried her hair. She donned a pair of tan trousers and a chocolate brown sweater. After putting on some lipstick she was about to leave the room when she remembered the label. She wanted to question Jim about it, and she slid it into her pocket. Then she left the room, locking the door behind her.

As Nancy walked down the hall she noticed that one of the doors was slightly ajar. She eased the door open and found Trish at the dresser, carefully folding clothes.

"What are you doing?" Nancy asked.

Trish gave a little yelp of surprise. "You scared me!" she cried.

"You still haven't answered my question," Nancy said.

"This is Michael's room, and I'm just packing up his things. No one's bothered to do that yet," Trish replied.

"How did you get in here?" Nancy asked her. "Did you have a key to his room?"

"As a matter of fact, no," Trish explained. "I

saw Mia here earlier, rummaging through Michael's things."

"What was Mia doing?" Nancy asked, perplexed.

"Certainly not packing up his stuff," Trish said sarcastically. "It looked like she was going through his papers."

The study notes! Nancy thought.

"After she left," Trish went on, "I checked the door and found she hadn't locked it. I came back later just to check things out and see if there was anything I could do for Michael."

"So Mia had a key?" Nancy asked.

"I guess so," Trish answered. "Michael probably gave it to her. After all, she *is* his *girlfriend!*"

"So what did you find?" Nancy said.

"She hadn't packed up any of his things," Trish muttered again, obviously agitated. She put the folded clothes into a suitcase that was open on the bed. She appeared to be in a kind of trance, as if nothing could be more important than this activity.

"I need to ask you a question," Nancy said after a moment. "I found this." She pulled the label from her pocket and handed it to Trish, watching closely to see her reaction. "Can you tell me what it is?"

Trish stopped folding clothes and reluctantly took the label and read it. "I don't know anything about it," she answered, shrugging.

"What if I told you that Michael may have been poisoned?" Nancy asked.

Trish's eyes widened. "Poisoned?" she repeated. Suddenly her eyes narrowed. "I get it," Trish said. "You think I had something to do with it!"

"I know that you used Matt," Nancy began, "so that you could be near Michael."

"How do you know that?" Trish said.

"I overheard your argument with Matt earlier," Nancy told her. "And Mia received a threatening phone call. Did you call her?" Nancy knew she was taking a gamble in laying out all her cards. But she needed to see Trish's reaction to the evidence.

Trish looked stunned. It took her a moment to find her voice. "I haven't threatened anyone!" she managed to say. She took a deep breath. "I certainly wouldn't threaten Mia."

"What about the label?" Nancy pushed.

Trish's eyed her carefully. "I told you, I don't have any clue about that. If you think for one minute that I would hurt Michael, you're dead wrong!" Trish put the last of Michael's things into his suitcase and zipped it shut. She picked it up and, without saying another word, carried it out of the room with her.

Nancy watched Trish leave. She couldn't tell if Michael's former girlfriend was telling the truth or not. She sighed in frustration.

Just then, Ned appeared at the doorway. "What are you doing in here?" he asked. "I was on my way to your room."

"I found Trish packing up Michael's things. She and I had a little conversation about the label and the threatening call to Mia."

"What did you find out?" he asked.

She told him about Trish's reactions to her questions. "I didn't really discover anything solid," Nancy continued. "All I know is that I have two suspects, but I don't have any hard evidence that points to either of them. It's not as if I caught anyone red-handed with the poison!" Nancy was perplexed. She had to find real proof that either Trish or Jim had poisoned Michael or called Mia, and she had to work quickly.

"I want to track Jim down and see if he knows anything about the label," Nancy said.

"Do you want me to come along?" Ned asked.

"Not now," she said. "I think I'd better do this one alone. I'll see you soon." She kissed Ned. "Don't worry."

She went to the front desk. Mrs. McVee told her that Jim was probably in the employees' break room.

Nancy followed Mrs. McVee's directions and found Jim putting on his jacket in front of an open locker. "I have a question for you," she said, startling him.

"Why should I talk to you?" he said brusquely. He slammed the locker shut.

Nancy took hold of his arm and stopped him. "Look, you haven't been at all cooperative, and that makes me think you're hiding something. Michael might have a bad case of the flu, but if it turns out somebody did something to put him in the hospital, I won't hesitate to throw suspicion onto you when the police come around. Are you going to talk to me or not?" She let go of his arm.

Jim looked resigned. "Okay, what's your question?" he asked, sitting down on a bench.

"I found this," she said, showing him the label. "Is anything containing poison used around the inn?"

Jim examined the label. He looked at her warily.

"I'm trying to rule out the possibility that Michael was accidentally poisoned," she said.

"Yeah, okay, we use some pretty heavy-duty cleaning stuff," he told her. "Even pesticides for the gardens."

"So how can you be certain Michael wasn't exposed to something like that?" Nancy asked.

"If you mean on the basis of this label, it's easy," Jim said. "We only purchase things in bulk sizes. This label is small, which means it probably came from some kind of small container—not something we'd buy."

Nancy had suspected as much. "Just one more thing," she said. "Can you show me the props and explain how things are set up for each scene?"

"You're really cutting into my free time now," Jim said, looking at his watch.

"It won't take long," Nancy told him.

Jim looked at her and heaved a sigh. "Come on," he said finally, heading for the door.

Nancy followed him down a hallway to a small storage room lined with shelves. A variety of items filled the shelves, and underneath each item was a number.

Jim pulled a clipboard off a hook on the wall and said, "The props for each play are numbered according to the scene." He showed her the clipboard. "I've got them listed here, so I can pull all the right props out easily."

Nancy glanced around the shelves. "Show me the props for last night," she said.

Jim checked his list, then motioned to one shelf. "There weren't many," he said. "Just what's on the tea service."

"Is that the same one you use for all the scenes?" Nancy asked, examining one of the cups from the tray. She hoped he hadn't noticed that one was missing.

"Yeah," Jim said. "It gets cleaned after every use, then put back here."

"Who does that?" Nancy asked.

"Usually the kitchen staff," he said. "They make the tea and whatever food they're serving in the scene."

"You said 'usually,'" Nancy observed. "Did someone else take care of it last night?"

Jim nodded. "The first night guests arrive, it's pretty hectic around here. Last night, I had to make the tea because somebody forgot. It was getting so late, I almost had to settle for cold, colored water!" Jim smiled.

Nancy was surprised to see him smile, but she smiled back. "How about the other stuff?" she asked. "You know, the lemon, sugar, and milk?"

"I'd gotten that done earlier," he answered. "I was afraid the milk was sour because I had left it out on the tray so long."

"Oh?" Nancy asked.

Jim's face clouded over. "Now I know what you're getting at!" he said. "You think the milk had something to do with your friend getting sick!" He shook his head and took the teacup from her hand. "If you'll excuse me," he said coldly, "I'm off duty now."

Before Nancy could stop him, he was out the door. She went back to the employees' break room, but he wasn't there.

Couldn't Jim be the culprit? Even though he had answered her questions, he could easily have put something in the milk. He must have access to the room keys, too, she thought. Maybe he planted that label in Trish's room. She took note of Jim's locker number and decided to take a look—later though, because she figured she would need Ned to act as a lookout for her.

"There you are!" Ned exclaimed as she was closing the door to the break room. "When you didn't come back right away I got nervous. Mrs. McVee said you might be here."

"I'm glad you're here," she said. "I have some things to tell you." Nancy took his hand and led him into a phone alcove in the hallway. There was no door, but Nancy thought it was private enough.

"What's going on?" Ned asked her.

She recounted her conversation with Jim. "So Trish might not have done it?" he asked.

"I'm not ruling out Trish," she told him.

"She seems to have a number of strikes against her," he said. "Hey, I think we should get over to the hospital."

"I need to get something. I'll meet you on the porch," she said.

"See you in a few." He left the alcove.

As Nancy was leaving she heard a soft noise and turned to see one of the doors in the hallway closing. Had someone been eavesdropping on her conversation with Ned? If so, that person was probably Jim, she thought.

Nancy ran to the door and pulled it open. From the light in the hallway, she could make out a large storage area used for nonperishable goods. She saw a brief flash of light across the room. Another door! She ran across the room, then stopped and opened the door just a crack. She saw a corridor leading to a delivery door. Directly across from her was a door to the kitchen. The corridor was deserted, and she didn't recognize anyone in the kitchen.

Frustrated, Nancy retraced her steps and headed to the front of the inn. She stepped out on the wraparound porch and stopped, needing a moment to calm down.

Suddenly she felt something hard pressed against her back, and someone whispered hoarsely, "Stop right there."

Chapter

Eight

You're the next victim," the voice whispered.

Nancy froze, her heart pounding in her ears.

"Just give a big scream and fall down dead!"

Nancy stammered for a second—it took a moment for her to realize she wasn't in real danger—but then she let loose a bloodcurdling scream and fell over onto the ground.

Ned, who had been standing on the lawn talking to several friends, raced toward her, as did his friends.

Lying on the wooden floor, Nancy felt the vibrations of pounding feet and tried as hard as she could to keep from laughing. In an instant Ned was kneeling by her side, calling her name, obviously upset. He rolled her body over, and still Nancy kept her eyes closed and her face slack. But when he felt for her pulse, Nancy couldn't hold out any longer. She burst out laughing.

"What gives?" Ned asked, bewildered.

"I'm sorry," Nancy began, laughter making it difficult to speak. "I'm the next victim! I'm dead! It's not very funny with poor Michael in the hospital and everything, but still . . . I had you on the run!"

Everybody else started laughing too, and Ned shook his head and smiled thinly. "Your acting job was too good, Nan. You gave me a scare!"

She told the group about the voice and what had felt like a gun in her back.

"Could you tell who was speaking?" Tom Lodin, one of Ned's fraternity brothers, asked.

"No," Nancy answered. "Come to think of it, I couldn't even tell whether it was male or female."

"Great stunt," Matt Gervasio said. Everyone agreed, and one by one they drifted away.

"The cast must've wanted you out of the picture, after your little gazebo-rescue this afternoon," Ned said when they were alone. "You're messing up their plot."

"Or maybe I was getting too close to fingering the murderer." Nancy smiled.

"Now you'll just have to work on the Michael mystery," Ned said. "Speaking of which, we'd better get over to the hospital."

"You're right. I still have to pack up the teacup, though."

"Meet you at the car," Ned said as he jogged off.

Nancy headed inside. After getting the packing supplies she needed from Mrs. McVee, she hurried up the stairs but was distracted when she recognized the petite figure with blond hair in the sitting room at the top of the stairs, apparently resting.

"Hi, Trish," she said. Trish didn't turn around. Her hands were over her face, and Nancy could hear quiet sobbing.

"Just leave me alone," Trish said, her voice muffled by her hands. "I don't want to be around anyone right now."

"Is there something I can do?" Nancy asked, sitting next to her. Trish was a suspect, but she couldn't leave the girl here by herself.

"Nothing," Trish mumbled. She turned her back to Nancy. Nancy could hear her sniffling, so she took a tissue out of her pocket and reached around to offer it to her.

"Trish," Nancy said, "what is it?"

Trish took the tissue and turned to face Nancy. "I made a terrible mistake," she said, blowing her nose. "You wouldn't understand."

Nancy looked at her. "What did you do?"

Trish was staring down at her hands. "I really don't think you'll understand."

"Just try me," Nancy told her. She sensed some kind of confession coming.

"I wasn't there for him," Trish said, and a tear slipped down her cheek. "He needed me, and I wasn't there."

"Who needed you?" Nancy pushed.

Trish suddenly faced Nancy. "Michael, of course!" she said irritably. "Who did you think I meant?"

"Let's just back up. Why don't you tell me the whole story?" Nancy said.

"At the murder mystery that first night," Trish began, "I wasn't there for him when he was sick. There he was, lying on the floor suffering, and it was my fault."

Nancy stiffened. Here it is, she thought. "Your fault?" she asked.

"None of this would have happened if I was with him," she said.

"But you *were* there," Nancy said somberly. "You know the hat Mickey Sloan was wearing that night." She waited for Trish's reaction.

"I know," Trish said, not seeming to mind that she had been caught in a lie. "I was there at the beginning, but I left. I know I told you I didn't go, but the truth is, I just couldn't stay and watch him."

"How could you have stopped Michael from getting sick?" Nancy asked.

Trish looked at her sadly. "I'm his good luck

charm," she answered. "If I had stayed, this wouldn't have happened. Nothing bad ever happened to him with me around."

Good luck charm? Nancy thought about that for a moment. Trish really believed this; Nancy could see it in her face.

She realized she wasn't going to get anywhere if she let Trish continue talking about good luck charms, and she needed some concrete details. So she tried a different tack. "I don't think you could have prevented it," she said.

"You obviously have no respect for the mysterious bonds of love," Trish said, and stood up abruptly. "I've got to go. Thanks for the tissue."

"No problem," Nancy answered, and Trish left.

As Nancy walked to her room, she considered her odd conversation with Trish. Maybe Ned was right: Trish did seem to be somewhat unstable.

Once in her room, Nancy took the shoe box Mrs. McVee had given her and made a nest in it with the newspaper Mrs. McVee had also provided. Then she bent down and carefully removed the teacup from under her bed. She covered the top with aluminum foil, then gently placed it in the center of the nest. Last, she put the cover on the box.

After quickly brushing her hair and touching up her lipstick, Nancy grabbed her backpack, her raincoat, and the box, then left the room, locking the door behind her.

By now, gathering storm clouds had turned the sky gray and murky. She found Ned waiting in the driver's seat of her Mustang, drumming his fingers on the steering wheel.

"And did I say you could drive?" she asked him, grinning.

"I know this car is your baby," Ned answered. "But I know the way to the hospital. It'll be quicker if I drive. We haven't got much time to get there."

"Okay, but be careful," she said, tossing him the keys. "It's so overcast, it looks like the sky's about to open up. And I didn't notice any streetlights on the roads up here."

She walked around to the passenger side, got in, and fastened her safety belt. She threw her pack in the back and carefully held the box in her lap. "The teacup," Nancy explained when Ned looked at it questioningly.

As Nancy told Ned about Trish's behavior, the rain began to fall, first in a trickle, then in a downpour. They were now on the main road, and Nancy could barely make out anything ahead of them. Ned slowed down and switched on the headlights.

"It's not far from here," Ned said. "Once we get into town, there ought to be lights."

Nancy was gathering her thoughts about the questions she would ask Michael. She hoped the nurses would allow her enough time to talk to him. She had to find out what he knew about Jim and whether he thought that Trish could really be a danger to him and Mia. She wondered if she should mention that Mia and Trish had both been in his room.

Nancy looked up to see Ned glancing in the rearview mirror. "What's the matter?"

"Nothing. I just thought I saw some headlights behind us."

"The driving conditions are lousy with this rain," she said. "Just take it easy."

"Yes, dear," Ned said dryly.

Just then, the rearview mirror lit up, and Nancy turned to see a car behind them. "Whoever they are, they should turn off their high beams," she said. "The glare in the rearview mirror is really annoying!"

"It sure is," Ned answered, turning the mirror away from the lights. "They're going awfully fast around these turns."

Nancy turned again to look at the car behind them. It was gaining on them rapidly, and she wondered why it wasn't slowing as it approached. Ned gripped the wheel tightly.

"I hope they're not planning on passing us," he said, his voice tense. "The curve up here looks sharp."

Nancy was alarmed by Ned's tone. "Let them pass before the curve," she said. Ned eased up on the accelerator.

"They're right behind us, Ned," Nancy said. "Just keep steady."

Ned glanced in the sideview mirror. "They're going too fast!" he said. "Hold on—I'm pulling off the road before we get hit." He put on the brakes and veered off the road. The Mustang's tires skidded on wet gravel, and Ned pulled to a stop just as the other car zoomed past.

Nancy was gripping the shoe box tightly. "That was close!" she exclaimed, and took a deep breath to calm herself. "They must have seen us. Why didn't they slow down?"

"I don't know," Ned said, staring down the road as the car disappeared around the curve.

"Ned, what's the matter?" Nancy asked when she saw the expression on his face.

"Nan, you're not going to believe this," Ned said, "but that was Michael's car!"

Chapter

Nine

$\mathbf{M}$ICHAEL'S CAR?" Nancy asked, stunned.

"Yeah, but with all the rain, I couldn't see who was driving," Ned said.

They sat in silence for a moment, then Nancy said, "Since both Mia and Trish were in Michael's room, maybe one of them took the keys to his car."

"Whoever it is should know better. That car is Michael's baby," Ned said. "Do you think they were trying to run us off the road?"

That thought had occurred to her. She also wondered if someone had somehow figured out what was in the box and was trying to keep her from getting it to the hospital. "I'm not sure," she answered honestly.

Ned started the car and pulled out onto the road. He drove carefully, slowing at every curve.

Finally, they saw the turn up ahead that led to the main road. As they headed to the hospital, Nancy kept glancing around, hoping to see the red sports car parked along the way. When they arrived at the hospital entrance, she still hadn't spotted it.

"We're here," Ned said. "Safe and sound."

"Finally," Nancy replied. She gave a peek at her watch. "We'd better hurry. It's getting late, and we need to get back in time for dinner."

They hurried inside and found Michael's floor. Nancy left the shoe box with a nurse at the desk, who promised to be sure the cup got to Michael's doctor. The nurse said that Nancy and Ned could stay for ten minutes, but cautioned them not to tire Michael out.

"Hey, buddy," Ned said as he opened the door. "How are you feeling?"

"Like I got hit by a bus," Michael answered with a weak laugh. "Hey, Nancy," he waved at her, "it was nice of you to come."

"Hi, Michael," she answered. "You're looking good!"

"Oh, sure," he said. "But thanks anyway."

"Sorry we're here so late," Ned told him, "but we got held up on the way over."

"Those roads are so dark!" Nancy quickly cut in. She didn't want Michael to know about his car. He looked so ill, she didn't want to upset him.

"Michael," Nancy started, "I have a couple of questions for you, if you feel up to it."

"Sure," he responded. "Anything to take my mind off being here! Why don't you have a seat?" He motioned to the two visitors' chairs, and she and Ned sat down.

"Do you know a guy named Jim Haines?" she asked. "He goes to Emerson."

Michael thought for a moment. "Jim Haines," he said. "The name does ring a bell." He paused. "I think he was in my chemistry lab, spring semester."

"He also rushed the fraternity," Ned said.

Michael thought about that for a moment. "Oh, yeah," he said. "I remember now. Last year, wasn't it?"

"Yes, it was," Ned replied. "He seemed so angry and unfriendly, I couldn't figure out why he even bothered rushing."

"I couldn't figure that out either," Michael said. "Especially since he told us he couldn't commit any time to the Omega House activities and charities because of his job."

"So, you don't know him well?" Nancy asked.

"No, I don't," Michael answered. "I think I lent him some notes for a class he missed." Michael brightened. "Yeah, I did," he said, "because after the next exam, he accused me of giving him the wrong notes so he'd fail the test!"

"That sounds like the Jim Haines we've come to know and love," Ned commented.

"I just figured he didn't study enough and wanted someone to blame his failure on," Michael said.

"Did you ever talk to him again?" Nancy asked.

"No, I tried to steer clear of him," Michael told her. "He didn't seem like the kind of guy I'd like to hang around with."

"You can say that again," Ned muttered.

Nancy could see that Michael was tiring, and she didn't want to push him. "Just one more question," she said. "Then we'll go, so you can get some sleep. Do you think Trish would want to hurt you or Mia?"

Michael looked shocked. "Trish?" he asked. "Why would she want to hurt me? And what about Mia? Has something happened?"

Nancy explained about the phone call to Mia. As he listened, Michael went white. Nancy really didn't want to upset him, but she needed to find out what he thought.

"Trish wouldn't hurt anyone," Michael said. "She may have gone a bit crazy when we broke up, but she's not the type to threaten people."

"I thought you had to stop taking her calls," Nancy said. "She was annoying you and Mia."

"To tell you the truth," Michael said, "her calls didn't bother me as much as they bothered Mia. She's the reason I told Trish to leave me alone. Trish and I were trying to stay friends, and Mia said she didn't like that. I guess I sort of wimped out, but Mia and I were getting along so great! I just didn't want to blow it with her."

"Everyone thought Trish was really harassing you," Ned cut in, "and you mean she wasn't?"

"Well, she did go a little crazy for a while," Michael answered. "She gave Mia and me a hard time when she saw us together, but she's calmed down."

"One more thing," Nancy said. "What's Trish's major?"

"Her major?" Michael asked, suppressing a yawn. "Chemistry. As a matter of fact, she was in that class with Jim and me, too."

The nurse rolled a blood pressure monitor into the room and told them it was time to go. Nancy and Ned said their goodbyes and promised to visit again before they went back to Emerson. He smiled and waved weakly as they shut the door.

"A different story every time you talk to someone, huh?" Ned asked, as he and Nancy walked down the corridor.

"Yeah," she replied. "It's getting very confusing."

They stopped at the elevator, and Nancy glanced back down the corridor as she pressed the down button. She saw a girl coming out of a stairwell entrance. She stopped outside Michael's closed door.

"Trish?" Nancy called. Trish whirled around, her eyes huge with surprise.

"I—I thought you guys left," she stammered.

"What are you doing here?" Ned demanded.

She took one last glance at Michael's door, then walked down the corridor to where Nancy and Ned were standing. "I was desperate to see Michael, and I didn't want anyone to know. I figured all his visitors would be gone by now."

"How did you get here?" Ned asked.

"I took Michael's car," she said innocently.

Nancy and Ned looked at each other. So it was Trish who had run them off the road.

"You almost killed us on the way here!" Ned exclaimed.

Trish looked horrified. "I had no idea that was you," she managed to say.

"Why didn't you slow down when you got too close to us?" Nancy demanded.

"Michael's car has a manual transmission," Trish answered. "I've only driven those a few times, and before I knew it, the car was in a high gear, and I had to go fast so it wouldn't stall out. I never tried to hurt you!"

Nancy had her doubts about this. She looked to Ned for his input.

"Michael's car definitely has its quirks. I've had trouble driving it myself," Ned admitted.

"I got the keys from Michael's room earlier," Trish volunteered. "I didn't want anyone using it while he was gone."

Anyone but you, you mean, Nancy thought. "I think we'd better be going. Visiting hours are over."

"I didn't even get to see him," Trish said sadly.

"He was exhausted when we left," Ned said. "Maybe you could come back tomorrow," he added, "but get a ride from someone or take the bus. You're dangerous in that car."

"I will," Trish answered. "I'll be more careful on the way back tonight. I promise!"

"We'll follow you, just to make sure you get back in one piece," Ned said.

"One more thing," Nancy said. "If you were driving so fast, how come we got here *before* you did?"

Trish looked sheepish. "I whizzed right by the hospital and didn't realize it. Then I had to turn around and drive back."

Nancy nodded but didn't say anything. She'd have to give Trish the benefit of the doubt for now.

They left the hospital, and Nancy saw Michael's car parked in a dark corner of the parking lot. Trish really didn't want anyone to see her here, Nancy thought. They got into their cars and headed back to the inn.

"I think she was telling the truth," Ned said to Nancy, once they were on their way.

"Maybe she was telling the truth about the car, but what about the poison? As a chem major, she would have access to all kinds of dangerous stuff."

"I don't know," Ned said. "That's your department. Finding out the truth."

They rode the rest of the way back in silence. The rain had stopped, and Nancy could make out some stars in the clearing sky. As promised, Trish was driving slower and more carefully. They were able to follow her easily back to the inn. When they arrived, the inn was glowing with light, and a group of guys were playing a pre-dinner game of touch football on the wet lawn. Ned parked the Mustang next to Michael's car as Trish got out. She gave them a quick wave and went inside.

Ned already had his room key out, but he said to Nancy, "I think I'll join the game."

"I'll watch," Nancy said, catching the key he tossed to her and sitting down on a rocking chair on the porch.

About ten minutes later the game broke up, and Ned ran up the porch steps to Nancy. "I'm going to get cleaned up for dinner," he said.

"No problem," she responded. "I'll wait for you here."

As soon as Ned disappeared into the inn Nancy realized she had his key. Hurrying inside, she saw Ned at the top of the stairs. His friend Paul was on the landing. "Hey, Ned!" he shouted. "Catch."

Ned turned, caught the football, and as he turned back, he collided with Jim Haines, who was heading for the staircase, carrying a tray of room service dishes. Glasses, flatware, and dishes crashed to the ground.

"What do you think you're doing?" Jim screamed. "You're going to pay for this!"

"Hey, I'm sorry. I didn't see you," Ned told him. "I'll help clean it up." Ned bent down and reached for a broken glass. Behind him Paul started picking up some plates, which hadn't broken.

"Forget it!" Jim yelled. "I don't want help from any frat boys!" He pushed Ned's arm away.

Ned and Paul stood watching Jim toss cutlery and dishes onto the tray. "I'm really sorry," Ned said.

Jim stood, holding a steak knife he had picked up off the floor. "Sure you are," he spat.

"Come on," Ned insisted. "It's our fault. Let us clean up this mess."

"I said *leave me alone,*" Jim growled, punctuating each word with a wave of the knife.

As Nancy raced up the stairs, she saw the gleam of the knife as Jim thrust it toward Ned.

Chapter

Ten

"Ned!" Nancy yelled.

Jim stopped and turned toward Nancy. "Oh, great! Another little helper."

"It's okay, Nancy," Ned said, cautiously stepping away from Jim. "It looks like things just got out of hand here."

"I saw the knife," she said. "That definitely was getting out of hand."

"Knife?" Jim asked, looking down at his hand as if he suddenly realized he was holding it. "You can't think I was going to hurt anybody!"

"You got pretty close a couple of times," Ned told him.

Jim paled. He dropped the knife on the tray. "I didn't realize I was holding it," he said quietly. He quickly finished picking up the dishes, then stood, holding the tray.

Nancy bent over and retrieved a stray fork from the floor. "We won't say anything about this," she told Jim, placing the fork on the tray.

Jim squared his shoulders and glared at her. "That's big of you," he said flatly. He turned sharply and headed down the stairs.

"Are you sure we should let him go like that?" Paul asked.

"Yeah, I think it's okay," Ned answered. "He knows he overreacted and that he could lose his job if we told Mrs. McVee."

"I think we both should keep out of his way, but you're right, Ned," Nancy said. "He'll need to be a little more cooperative now that we have something on him."

"Yeah. And what *we* need is dinner!" Ned announced in an effort to lighten up the mood.

"Dr. Nickerson's cure-all—food!" Nancy said, laughing. She realized she was hungry, and after Ned had washed up, they went down to the dining room. They sat at a table in the back for some privacy and began looking over the menu.

"I love how they offer three appetizers, three entrees, and three desserts for dinner," Nancy commented, scanning the list.

"Me, too," Ned said. "When you have a choice between a main dish of meat, pasta, or fish, it doesn't take long to decide what you want— especially when you're starving!"

Nancy laughed. "Well, if you can catch the

waiter's eye and tell him we're ready to order, you'll have your dinner that much sooner."

After they had ordered, Nancy pulled her chair close to Ned's. "That's better," she said.

"I completely agree," he responded, putting his arm around her. When the waiter brought their sodas, Nancy took the straw from her glass and added it to Ned's.

"Have a sip," she said. They both leaned in to take a drink. Their heads knocked together, and they started laughing.

"It always seemed so romantic to share a soda in those old movies!" Nancy exclaimed, rubbing her head. "Maybe I'd better take my straw back," she told him. "This kind of romance hurts!"

They were both still smiling when Nancy looked up and saw Mia enter the room.

"There's Mia," she said, pointing to the doorway. "Can I ask her to join us?"

"Sure," Ned said. "Just don't invite her to add her straw to my soda!"

Nancy giggled. "I won't." She waved at Mia. The girl nodded, said something to the woman behind the hostess desk, then came over to join them.

"I wasn't planning on having dinner down here," Mia said as she approached the table. "I only took a minute to come down and order something to bring back to my room. It's quicker than waiting for room service."

"Well, sit down for a second, anyway," Nancy said. She pulled over a chair for Mia.

"I talked to Trish earlier," Nancy began, "and she said she saw you in Michael's room looking through his things."

"I needed to get the notes," Mia answered. "He didn't have a chance to give them to me before he got sick. Besides," she added, "what was Trish doing, checking up on me? She's caused enough trouble as it is."

Before Nancy could respond, the waiter came to the table, carrying their appetizers. Mia stood up as he placed the plates in front of them.

"I'll be out of your way now," Mia said.

"Hey, we're going to the hospital tomorrow before heading back to campus," Ned said. "Why don't you come with us?"

"Maybe I will," she answered, and walked away.

"That was strange," Nancy commented.

"What?" Ned asked, taking a bite of his baked clams.

"She didn't sound too anxious to go to the hospital," she said.

"No, she didn't," Ned replied. "But maybe she's made other plans already."

"Or maybe she'd like to see Michael alone, without us tagging along."

Nancy glanced over at Mia. She had been waiting at the hostess station for her food and now was carrying a tray out of the dining room. Nancy saw a quick movement out of the corner of her eye. Jim Haines was hurrying out of the dining room—in hot pursuit of Mia!

Nancy sprang up from her seat, and Ned followed without question. They both left the table and followed Jim into the hallway. They stopped when they saw that Jim had Mia cornered.

"Your boyfriend organized this weekend," Jim was saying, "so you'll have to take care of it!"

Mia looked frightened. "Leave me alone!" she said. She clutched her tray tightly.

"Hey!" Nancy shouted. "Stop it!"

Jim whirled around and glared at Nancy. "Not again! This is none of your business."

"What do you think you're doing?" she demanded.

"Her boyfriend messed up the amount of the deposit, so I'm just letting her know I'm not about to let anybody shortchange Mrs. McVee."

Now Ned was furious. "That's been taken care of," he said. "Check with Mrs. McVee. She'll tell you!"

"Oh. Well, she's been cheated before. She's not that great at looking after the small details," Jim said tersely. He turned and walked back toward the dining room.

"Are you okay?" Nancy asked Mia.

"Fine," Mia answered, still shaky. "That guy's

got one hot temper!" she said, managing a small laugh. She excused herself.

"Jim is really out of control," Ned said.

"Maybe his temper will make him slip up and give me the proof I need to nail him," Nancy said. "In the meantime, let's enjoy our dinner."

They went back to their seats. They finished their appetizers, and their main courses were served. Olivia and Mrs. Wendham stopped at each table, chatting with the guests. When they reached Ned and Nancy, Mrs. Wendham checked that they were enjoying themselves, then moved to the next group. Olivia stayed behind, taking a seat with them.

"Is Michael all right?" she asked Nancy anxiously.

"Getting better," Nancy said, taking a bite of her chicken Dijon.

"I'm so relieved," Olivia said. "He scared me terribly!"

"Us too," Ned answered.

Nancy had a thought. "Olivia, can you tell me about Jim Haines?" she asked.

"Jim?" Olivia asked. "You mean the guy who handles the props?"

"That's the one," Nancy answered. "Have you known him long?"

"Sorry, but no," Olivia said. "Actually, I've worked here for only a month. We were in rehearsal for three weeks, and this is the first play I've been in."

"Can you give me any idea what Jim's like?" Nancy asked.

Olivia thought for a moment. "I know he's Mrs. McVee's right hand around here. He has access to everything. But I don't know him well. We've mostly just talked about the play. He's a little on the brusque side—a hotheaded redhead like me," she said with a laugh.

"Hardly like you, Olivia," Ned offered.

Nancy shot Ned a look as Olivia stood to continue her tour of the dining room. "I've got to get back to 'Mother.'" She gave them a wink.

"Thanks for your time," Nancy said, as Olivia moved off toward Mrs. Wendham.

"If he has access to everything," Ned started, "then he could have gotten into Trish's room and planted that poison label."

"Exactly what I was thinking," Nancy answered. "Although it doesn't make much sense. Why would he expect anyone to look for it?"

"I see what you mean," Ned said. "Maybe he's going to find some way to accuse her—then have someone search her room."

"I suppose that's a possibility," Nancy said doubtfully.

"I'm sure he didn't count on Detective Drew finding it," Ned said.

They were just finishing dessert when Mrs. McVee walked into the dining room. "Will everyone please remove their menus from the folders in which they've been placed." There was much rustling as people took the menus out of the folders. "If you'll turn over your menus, you'll find a search warrant on the back. You are all invited to accompany Detective Ryan on a search of the suspects' rooms after dinner. Secret clues in the rooms might point to the murderer. Please note that you must visit, in order, the rooms on your menu. That will avoid having everyone in the same room at one time."

Ned jumped up from the table. "Come on, Nancy! This will be great—for me, anyhow. Unfortunately for you, you're dead and can't compete for the prize. Now you'll just have to be Watson to my Holmes, eh, what?"

Nancy rolled her eyes. "Fine, Sherlock. I've been too distracted to be much of a threat to you in this contest anyhow," she admitted as they followed several other couples to their first stop, Mickey Sloan's room.

Mickey's room was decorated much like Nancy's, with pale yellow flowered wallpaper and a coordinating bed set. Ned immediately found what appeared to be the first clue: a hacksaw under the bed.

"Excellent," he said, a look of satisfaction on his face.

They continued on to Jeffrey's room, which was very small and dark.

"Suitable for the help, I guess?" Nancy suggested.

They had to wait until the first group came out. A beaming Matt left the room and came toward them. "Here's a hint," Matt offered. "Don't forget to look in the drawer of the writing table!"

"This is like a scavenger hunt," Ned said, laughing as he and Nancy entered the room. Several other couples followed. Ned went straight to the writing table and opened the drawer. Sure enough, there was a note. He left it where it was and Nancy moved beside him to read it: "Keep your nose out of things that aren't any of your business, and keep what you know to yourself; it doesn't concern you."

"Well?" Nancy prompted, looking up at Ned. "Does this fit in with your theories, Detective?"

"We'll see," Ned replied.

The next room they stopped in was spacious and lavishly decorated. There was a huge bouquet of flowers on a dressing table, as well as perfume bottles and a silver brush-and-mirror set. A pink dressing gown was draped across the back of a chair.

"Hmmm, you'd think this room would have gone to a *paying* guest," Ned said.

Tucked behind the dressing table mirror was an insurance policy that revealed the outrageous amount of money Mrs. Wendham would receive if her diamonds were stolen.

Nancy noticed the Detective Ryan character

jotting notes in a small black book as everyone traveled from room to room.

In Robert Jones's room, Lynn Farber, Tom's girlfriend, gave an excited shriek as she picked up a plush seat cushion and found a diamond engagement ring.

"True love, or what?" Nancy asked.

"Oh, who knows? I'm confused at the moment," Ned said, as they followed Lynn and Tom to the last of the rooms on the tour.

There, in Olivia's room, a message was scrawled on the bathroom mirror in red lipstick. It read, "Your mother's hiding something."

Nancy and Ned exchanged a look. "So, what do you think?" Nancy asked.

"I think I'll reserve my judgment for the next scene," he said.

"It's not like you to keep secrets," she said as they left the room. Around them Nancy could hear other couples discussing the clues.

"No secrets," Ned replied. "I have to admit I originally thought the thief was Waverly, with his debt and company embezzlement hanging over his head. But his murder killed that idea. Now I'm trying to think like you. You know, looking at all the evidence and piecing it together."

Nancy thought about Ned's comment. There were so many pieces to the real mystery going on at the Old Pine Inn, she couldn't put it together—not yet, anyway. Michael was still lying in the hospital, and she was no closer to finding out who poisoned him than she was yesterday. And, especially after the phone call to Mia, she didn't need a lab to tell her that the oily film on the tea was poison. Time was running out, and Nancy was feeling the pressure. Yet she knew there was nothing more she could do that night.

"It's about time for bed," she said to Ned, "but I'm too wound up to sleep. How about a walk around the lake?"

"Sounds great," he answered.

Nancy got her leather jacket and then she and Ned, walking hand in hand, headed to the water. They stopped at a big rock that jutted over the lake, and Ned suggested they sit there for a while.

"It's so peaceful," Nancy said. She snuggled up next to Ned, who put his arm around her. They remained sitting there until Nancy began to shiver.

"You're getting cold," Ned said, hugging her close. "Let's head back."

Inside, they saw a few couples in the parlor and heard laughter coming from the game room in the back.

"Sounds like they're having a good time," Nancy commented.

"Yeah," Ned said, yawning, "but I'm too tired to check it out."

As Nancy and Ned climbed the wide stairs the

lights flickered, then went out completely, plunging the entire inn into darkness.

"Ned?" Nancy called out softly.

Suddenly someone grabbed Nancy from behind and, giving her a hard push, sent her tumbling down the stairs.

Chapter

Eleven

NANCY!" Ned called out. "Nancy, are you all right?" There were shrieks from the parlor as the lights flickered on, off, then on again.

Nancy was lying in a heap at the bottom of the stairs, and Ned raced down the stairs to her side.

"I'm fine," she said and managed to stand up. "Someone pushed me down the stairs. Did you see anybody?"

"No, no one," Ned said. "It was just too dark. I heard one of the waiters talking about some electrical problem earlier—a short in the basement or something. Whatever caused the blackout, it gave someone an opportunity to attack you. Are you sure you're okay?"

"My knee hurts, but that's all. I just bruised it, I think."

"This is getting more and more serious, Nan. I think we should call the police."

"No, we can't until we have actual proof that Michael was poisoned," Nancy said. "And, obviously my fall was no accident—someone deliberately pushed me, but neither of us saw anyone." She shook her head. "For now we're on our own, Ned."

"Okay. But I don't like this at all."

Ned helped Nancy into the parlor and eased her down onto a small couch in front of a still-glowing fire in the fireplace. He propped her leg up on the coffee table and slid a throw pillow beneath it.

"Is that better?" he asked, concerned.

"Thanks, Ned, much better now."

Several people came over and asked what had happened. "I'm just a klutz," Nancy said, laughing. "I fell down the stairs when the lights went out."

Nancy and Ned sat together talking softly for a while, enjoying the quiet of the night and the glow of the fire.

"Not quite the romantic weekend we'd planned, is it Nan?" he said, smiling.

"No," Nancy agreed, touching his face gently with her hand. "But—"

Just then Mia, carrying a notebook, entered the parlor. She walked over to Nancy and Ned. "Phew! I'm so glad the lights came back on. I was in my room studying and thought I'd have to quit for the night."

"Mia, a body's got to sleep!" Ned exclaimed. "Even Michael never studies this much, and he manages to ace test after test."

"I know," she said, settling into a comfortable chair. "That's why he's held on to the number one premed position all the way through to our senior year. He's a natural."

"I sure hope he can make up whatever he misses so he won't throw his chances for medical school," Ned said.

"Well, the thing is, most of the required classes are only offered at set times during the year, or during the four years, to be more accurate," Mia explained. "This is about the worst time for Michael to be in the hospital. If he falls behind, he may have to drop a required course, which means he'll have to delay applying to medical school."

"I'm sure he'll be well soon," Ned said.

"Bedtime for me," Nancy said, yawning.

"Me, too," Ned said. "Coming up, Mia?"

"I think I'll just finish some notes down here," she said as Ned helped Nancy to her feet.

Mia saw Nancy wince. "You okay?" she asked, eyeing the knee Nancy was clearly favoring.

"Volleyball," Nancy said, not wanting to discuss her attack. "Good night, Mia."

Ned helped Nancy up the stairs and walked

her to her room. "Now you're sure you'll be all right?" he asked with a grin.

"Yes, Nickerson, I'm fine. Now good night."

He pulled her close and held her for a moment, then kissed her. "Good night, Nancy," he said softly. "Breakfast at eight?"

"See you there," she whispered. Nancy let herself into her room and closed the door behind her. She took her nightgown out of a drawer, then decided she didn't want to go to sleep with her knee so stiff. She would go down to the kitchen for some ice—nobody would try to attack her again that night, she felt sure of that. She let herself out of the room, locking the door behind her.

Downstairs she peeked into the parlor. Mia wasn't there. Nancy walked down a hallway to the kitchen, where she turned on the lights and looked around for a plastic bag. She found one and then opened the large industrial freezer. She filled the bag with ice, then sat on a stool, pulled up her pants, and held the ice on her swollen knee.

She was startled when the kitchen doors opened and Jim Haines walked in.

"What's going on?" he demanded. "I was about to leave when I saw the lights on in here. What's with the knee?" he asked, noticing the ice bag.

"Oh, you don't know?" Nancy asked. Afraid Jim had been the one to push her, she felt her heart pounding but was determined not to show her apprehension.

"I have no idea. What are you talking about?"

Nancy had seen plenty of Jim's angry looks before, but she was surprised by his mild expression now. For once, he didn't appear menacing. In fact, she thought, he seemed genuinely concerned. Still, she was cautious.

"I fell in the blackout," she said simply.

"Sorry. I just checked out the fuse box in the basement, actually. We'll have to wait for the repair service to make sure the power's okay," he said. "Look, I wanted to talk to you anyway. I want you to know that I didn't hurt anyone," he told her. "I know you don't believe me, but it's true."

"Your track record so far makes me doubt you," she said, repositioning the ice on her knee. "Why bother to tell me this?"

"I got to thinking about how I've been acting," he said, nervously. "I realize I could be in big trouble if you guys ratted on me for that stupid knife thing, and I wanted you to know I appreciate that you didn't tell."

Nancy was blown away. Bad-tempered Jim was actually thanking her for something! "You're welcome," she said.

"I know it's not a good excuse, but I've been putting in a lot of hours, and I'm already getting behind in my classes. Then, this afternoon two people didn't show up, and I got stuck doing room service, which isn't part of my job. If there's anything you need, just let me know how I can help."

Did this guy have a split personality? Nancy wondered. After the angry encounters she had had with him, she was concerned about being alone with him—even if he was being nice at the moment. He was too much of a wild card.

"I really have to get to bed," she told him. "Ned's expecting me to say good night," she added, thinking it might be a good idea to have Jim believe Ned was expecting her. "Thanks for your offer." She pulled down her pants leg, then hobbled off, leaving him standing in the kitchen.

"It gets stranger by the minute," she said to herself as she climbed painfully up the stairs.

She reached her room and unlocked the door. She was awfully tired now and just wanted to crawl into bed. She headed into the bathroom to wash her face and brush her teeth. When she flipped on the light, she gasped.

Scrawled across the mirror was a message written in red lipstick: "Next time I won't miss!"

Chapter

Twelve

NANCY STARED at the words written on the mirror. She wasn't frightened, just curious about the message. And in a way, she felt oddly pleased. I must be getting close, she thought, because now the would-be killer is getting desperate. It was enough before to threaten Mia, but now they had to threaten *her!* She noticed a smudge across the bottom of the message, as if something had been dragged across it.

"That's ten points off for sloppiness," she said to herself, smiling. Her smile faded when she opened her kit bag to get her toothbrush. She found her favorite red lipstick open and smushed, all the way to the bottom of the tube. Now she recognized the color of the red lipstick on the mirror.

"Not only do I get threatened," she said aloud, "but now I have no lipstick!"

Nancy shoved a chair under her doorknob, just in case anyone tried to get in. Then she put on her nightgown and got under the covers. The events of the day had wiped her out, and she dropped off to sleep almost immediately.

Nancy woke to a stream of sunlight on her face. She looked at the clock and jumped out of bed, anxious not to miss breakfast with Ned, especially since she had a lot to tell him. She showered, only glancing at the lipstick threat. Then she dressed in a denim miniskirt and white turtleneck and hurried downstairs.

Ned was pacing in the lobby. "I've been waiting for you," he said. "I was getting worried."

"Am I late?" she asked. "Well, let's grab some breakfast. I'm starved, and I have a lot to tell you."

Ned looked at her, puzzled. "What do you mean by that?" he asked. "Wasn't I the one who walked you safely to your room last night?"

They picked out some pastries and fruit from the breakfast buffet and then sat at a quiet corner table. Nancy told Ned about her chat with Jim and about the message on the mirror.

"You're not kidding you had a lot to tell me!" he exclaimed.

"You know this means I'm getting closer," she

said between bites. "Time is running out, and both the would-be killer and I know it!"

"Look, Nan," he said, "I don't want you to get hurt. How about if I tag along with you today? You shouldn't be alone."

"Thanks, Ned," she said, smiling. "I'll take you up on that. I need to check out Jim's locker sometime today while he's working. You can be the lookout."

Ned quickly agreed.

Nancy took a sip of her coffee and stared into space. "You know," Nancy said, "that message on my mirror is a lot like what was going on in the play yesterday. Remember?"

"Yeah," Ned said. "Kind of weird, isn't it?"

"Yes, it is," Nancy said.

"It rules Jim out," Ned said. "He wouldn't have seen the show."

Nancy was silent for a moment. Then she said, "No, it doesn't rule him out. He handles all the props, which would include the lipstick. So he knows every scene. And he probably has access to master keys. . . ."

"I'm sorry to say that that may not be much of a clue," Ned said. "Master keys would probably be kept in Mrs. McVee's office. And having spent a fair amount of time there, I can tell you that she usually leaves the office open, even when she isn't there."

"So, what you're saying is anyone could have

gotten hold of the keys." Nancy groaned. "That's great, just great."

Just then Mrs. Wendham, sitting at a table close to the buffet, began to speak in a loud stage voice about the proper preparation of eggs Benedict, indicating that a scene was beginning. She wore a long string of pearls over her crisp white blouse. Mickey, standing nearby and filling her plate from the buffet, looked pale in a stylish cream-colored suit.

Jeffrey entered from the kitchen door and tended to Olivia, who was sitting beside Mrs. Wendham. Robert Jones pulled his chair closer to Olivia at the table.

"Olivia, stop fidgeting," said Mrs. Wendham.

"Mother, Derek Waverly is dead, and who knows who might be next?" Her face was pale, except for the peach-toned lipstick she wore.

Mickey spoke. "That's a lovely shade of lipstick, Olivia. Not your usual color, is it?"

Olivia shifted uncomfortably in her seat. "No, I've suddenly run out of my usual shade, and someone here knows it," she said, agitated. She turned to face her mother. "Tell me your big secret, Mother," she demanded. "I know you're keeping something from me!"

Mrs. Wendham fanned her face with a menu. "I don't know *what* you're talking about. Please pass the preserves."

Jeffrey was serving coffee at the table. Robert gave him a wary look. "Seen any good movies lately, Jeffrey?" he asked. Mrs. Wendham looked at them both, puzzled.

"You shouldn't bother him while he's working," she chided. "And what is wrong with you people? Yes, there's been another murder, but we can't start suspecting one another!"

"Who better to suspect?" Jeffrey asked.

All the players stood up at once and went to sit with other guests, as if they'd suddenly realized they didn't like the company they were keeping. Jeffrey walked by the table where Ned and Nancy sat.

"Hey, Jeffrey," Ned began. "Tell me, are Mrs. Wendham's affairs in order? That is, is she secretly in need of money?"

"Absolutely not," Jeffrey replied. "Lucky for me, because I've been saving my paycheck for some time, hoping to go on a cruise and have someone wait on me for a change," the butler said dryly, before walking on.

Ned laughed.

"You're totally into this, aren't you?" Nancy observed.

"Oh, yeah. I think I'm getting close, too. Hey, Mrs. Wendham!" he called.

She strolled over. "Hay is for horses, young man," she chided.

"Sorry. I have got two important questions for you, though. First, are you an only child?"

"No."

"Okay," Ned said, leaning forward in his

chair. "Now, is your maiden name Harriman?" he asked.

"Why, yes, it is!" Mrs. Wendham exclaimed, visibly flustered. She hurried away to another table.

Nancy studied Ned's face. "I have to admit, you sure look as though you're onto something, Nickerson."

"Yep. One more question should do it," he said, waving Mickey Sloan over.

"One question, Mickey. Is your mother living?"

"No, I'm sorry to say she is deceased," Mickey replied sadly.

"That's great news!" Ned said. "Oh, I mean, I'm sorry about your mother and everything."

Mickey patted Ned on the shoulder and leaned in to speak quietly. "Don't worry," she said. "It's only pretend, remember?" She flashed her green eyes at him and walked away.

Ned sat there looking extremely satisfied.

"I'm not even going to ask because I know you won't tell me," Nancy said, finishing up the last of her apple Danish.

"That's right. You'll have to wait just like everyone else to learn the results of my brilliant sleuthing."

"I'm sitting on the edge of my seat." She laughed, then stood up. "But meanwhile, I'm going to get a sweater so we can do something outside, okay?"

"Sounds good, Nan. I'll meet you out front."

Nancy dashed upstairs, unlocked her door, and went into the bathroom. She had left the message on the mirror so she could take more time to examine it after breakfast. Once again, she faced the mirror. This time, though, the only thing she saw was her own reflection. The message had disappeared!

The mirror had been wiped clean. All traces of the lipstick were gone. Nancy quickly checked her makeup bag. Her empty lipstick tube was still there.

"They forgot to take all the evidence," she murmured. She put the tube into her skirt pocket for safekeeping.

Why would they erase the message? Probably so that I'd know they could get into my room any time, she thought. Just showing me they really can get me if they want to. She shuddered. This was more serious than she had thought. She quickly brushed her teeth, grabbed her shoulder bag, then went downstairs to meet Ned.

Ned was waiting for her in the lobby. He gave her a kiss. "How about some croquet?"

Nancy gave him a quizzical look. "Croquet? You want to play croquet?"

"Well, I thought we should try every sport they've got here, and even though we won't break a sweat, croquet counts."

"I hate to be responsible for breaking your sports record," Nancy said, "but there's been a change in plans. When I went back to my room, I discovered that someone had been in there while we were at breakfast. The lipstick message was erased."

"Maybe it was the maid," Ned suggested.

"It couldn't have been because the bed wasn't made yet," Nancy said.

Ned gave Nancy a serious look. "I don't like this at all."

"Neither do I," she said. "I need to get to the bottom of this—and soon."

"How can I help?" Ned asked.

"I think it's time to check out Jim's locker," she said. "People are still finishing breakfast, so Jim should be busy for a while yet."

She led Ned down the hall to the break room. "What are you expecting to find?" he asked.

"I'll know when I find it," she said.

The door to the break room was open, and Nancy saw two employees closing their lockers and talking. Nancy pulled Ned around a corner, and they waited until the employees left.

"You stay at the entrance and watch," she said to him as she opened the door and looked inside. It was empty. "If anyone comes, let me know—quick."

"Ready when you are," Ned told her. He shut the door and stood just outside it.

Nancy located Jim's locker, pulled her lock-picking kit out of her shoulder bag, and quickly snapped open the lock. Jim's leather jacket was hung neatly on a hook, his extra shoes were lined up perfectly on the bottom, and a comb and some aftershave were in a small metal basket suspended from the shelf.

"Tidy guy," she muttered. She checked the pockets of his jacket, but they were empty. His backpack was on the other hook, but she didn't find anything suspicious in it. She ran her hands along the sides of the locker, but found nothing taped up or hidden away. The metal basket hung from a shelf at the top. The shelf was above her eye level, and she was standing on tiptoe when Ned opened the door.

"Somebody's coming," he whispered.

"Just a second," she answered. "I'm almost through."

She still couldn't see to the back of the shelf, so she did a wide sweep of the shelf with one hand. She hit something, and it clanked against the locker wall. She felt around again.

"Nan," Ned called softly over his shoulder to her, "we're going to have company."

"I'm just about done," Nancy said, and grabbed hold of the object from the shelf. She saw Ned out of the corner of her eye. He was coming toward her with a finger to his lips and pointing to a dark corner behind the last row of lockers. Nancy quickly snapped the locker shut and redid the lock. Ned took her arm, and they rushed behind the set of lockers.

The door opened, and Nancy heard two people

talking as they went to their lockers. Ned and Nancy were quiet until they heard the voices fade away and the door shut behind them.

"What did you find?" Ned asked.

Nancy stepped out into the light of the room. She opened her hands to show Ned a large ring of keys. Nancy examined them closer. They were marked with room numbers or names.

"What are those?" Ned asked her.

"These are the master keys to open every door at the inn."

Chapter

Thirteen

W<small>HY WOULD</small> J<small>IM</small> have them in his locker?" Ned asked.

"That's what I'm going to find out," Nancy said grimly. She led the way to the dining room, where they found Jim sorting silverware at one of the waiter stations.

"I need to talk to you for a minute," she said.

Jim stopped sorting. "Just a sec," he said. He called out to one of the waiters to take over for him while he took a short break.

"What's up?" he asked her after they retreated to the hallway.

"I found these," Nancy told him, and held out the set of keys.

"Where did you get them?" Jim asked. "They've been missing since Friday, and Mrs. McVee has been in a panic!"

Nancy studied him carefully. "I found them in your locker."

"What were you doing snooping in my stuff?" Jim demanded. "After I talked to you last night, you're still trying to pin something on me?"

"What were you planning to do with these?" Nancy asked. "Leave me another message?"

"What message?" Jim asked. "I told you before, I didn't do anything!" he said angrily.

"I know what you've said," Nancy started, "but these seem to suggest differently." She jangled the keys in front of him.

Jim took a step toward her. "I wouldn't do that if I were you," Ned said calmly but forcefully.

Jim stopped and stood where he was. He opened his hands in a gesture of helplessness. "Why would I have these in my locker?" he asked Nancy. "I can get them from Mrs. McVee's office any time I want. Someone must have put them there."

"You wouldn't want to rely on getting them from Mrs. McVee's office if you planned on breaking into someone's room at a specific time, would you?" Nancy stared directly at him.

"Listen," Jim said, "you've got to stop accusing me of this crazy stuff. Mrs. McVee trusts me, and I don't want you lying to her." He was breathing deeply, trying to keep himself under control. "I'm going back to work now, the work that I do very well, very reliably. And I don't want to hear any more about this." With that, he walked back into the dining room.

"No matter what he tells me," Nancy said, "these keys in his locker only strengthen the case against him."

"Yeah," Ned said. "With his temper, who knows what he might do." He paused for a moment, then asked, "What next?"

"I'd like to see Michael again. I have more questions for him, and I want to find out if the doctors have discovered anything." She looked at her watch. "It's too early, though. How about if we just knock a tennis ball around for a while? It'll help me clear my head."

"Another sport down!" Ned laughed.

Together they walked to the lobby. As they passed the main parlor they saw Mia, sitting on a couch, surrounded, as usual, by books and papers.

"She must be pretty down," Ned said, "spending all her time alone this weekend."

"You're right," Nancy said.

"We'll fix that," Ned said. "Hey, Mia!" Ned called to her. "You want to go to the tennis courts with us?"

She looked up from her book. "Sorry. I have a couple more chapters to go through." She smiled. "Thanks anyway."

"Well, don't forget our offer to take you to the hospital later."

"We'll see how the work goes," Mia said. "I do have a present to give Michael, though, so why don't you stop by my room after lunch? Mrs. McVee knits sweaters, and I bought him one to cheer him up."

"Oh, that's sweet, Mia. I'm sure it'll boost his spirits," Nancy said.

Ned went to the desk and picked up tennis rackets and a can of tennis balls. He was swishing one racket around, hitting imaginary shots. "Ready?" he asked Nancy.

"Set," she said. They said goodbye to Mia and went out to their game.

For about half an hour, Nancy and Ned hit the ball back and forth. With each shot, Nancy was lining up pieces of the case in her mind. She thought about Trish and Jim, and all the evidence that was piling up against them. Matt and Jeff joined them after a while, and they played some doubles. When they finished, they went back to the inn to return the equipment.

Ned looked at his watch. "Do you want to have lunch now?" he asked. "The dining room just opened, but I'm already kind of hungry."

"Sounds good," Nancy said. "That way we can get to the hospital a little earlier."

"I need some carbohydrates today," she told Ned as they headed toward the buffet. "I'm feeling deprived."

"You're in luck," he replied. "I see a pasta

salad with vegetables. No red sauce to stain your nice white shirt!"

Nancy socked him on the arm. "I don't drop pasta on my clothes," she said. "My manners are impeccable. It's you we have to watch out for!"

Sure enough, halfway through lunch, Ned dropped a piece of pasta on his shirt. "I told you so!" Nancy said, and they laughed.

They finished eating, then strolled out of the dining room. "I missed having a murder mystery scene during lunch, but it was nice to have your undivided attention for a change," Nancy said.

Ned put his arm around her as they walked. "You know you're the most important thing on my mind," Ned assured her.

"Sure, as long as you have a full stomach," Nancy teased.

Out in the lobby, several guests were gathered around Detective Ryan. "I want you all to know that we now believe we have a culprit," he declared. "The murderer will be named at three o'clock this afternoon, so don't be late." He puffed out his chest importantly. "You'll all have an opportunity to assist me by telling me who you think is the killer. See you at three." The detective swaggered out through the front door.

"Well, Sherlock? Think you'll have it by then?" Nancy asked.

"Are you kidding? Get that detective back here, and I'll tell you right now!" he said.

Nancy laughed, but she felt anxious about her own case. She had very little time left. "How about if we go to the hospital right now?" Nancy asked. "That way we can be back in time for you to show off your brilliant sleuthing."

"Good idea. I can also talk to Michael about the final payment for the weekend, poor guy, and about what he wants me to do with his car."

"Okay. Let me run upstairs first, though, and see if Mia wants to come with us. I'll be right back."

Nancy bounded up the stairs. She was heading down the corridor when she heard a shriek coming from Mia's room. What now? Nancy wondered, running down the deserted hallway.

Mia's door was ajar, and Nancy raced inside. Mia was sitting on the bed, phone in hand. She was shaking and on the verge of tears. "What's wrong?" Nancy cried.

"It happened again." Mia moaned. She looked down at the receiver. "This time they said they would kill me."

Nancy took the receiver out of Mia's hand and hung it up, then sat down beside her. "Tell me exactly what they said."

"That's it—they said that they would kill me," Mia answered. She dabbed at her eyes. She was almost as pale as her white shirt.

"Did you recognize the voice?" Nancy asked.

"No," Mia began, "I couldn't tell who it was,

but I'm sure it was the same person who called before."

Nancy went to get Mia a glass of water and some tissues from the bathroom. "Come on, let's get out of this room, okay?" Nancy said. "I bet you'll feel better if we go see Michael. Ned's downstairs in the lobby waiting for us."

Mia agreed, and after she'd splashed water on her face and regained her composure, she picked up a shopping bag containing the sweater, and they left the room together. As they walked down the wide stairs they were surprised to see Ned standing with a uniformed police officer and another man.

Nancy glanced over at Mia, who looked alarmed. "Let's see what's going on," Nancy said, walking over to join them.

Ned turned as he heard them walk up behind him. His face was ashen.

"What's wrong?" Nancy asked.

Ned looked grim. "You were right, Nancy," he said. "Michael was poisoned."

131

Chapter

Fourteen

I'M SORRY it turned out I was right," Nancy said, taking Ned's hand. Mia remained behind.

"Detective Dean and Officer Vargo, I'd like you to meet Nancy Drew," Ned said. "She's the one who took the cup Michael was drinking from to the hospital."

"Ah, so *you're* the PI Michael talked about," the detective said, grinning. "Well, he owes you a big debt of gratitude. The chemical that was used to poison him is undetectable in the body. It was only when we sent the cup to the police lab for testing that our hospital laboratory was able to isolate the poison. Good work!"

Nancy smiled. "What's most important is how Michael's doing."

"He's been given an antidote, and he should be back on his feet in a few days."

Nancy breathed a sigh of relief. They still didn't know who the culprit was, but at least Michael was out of danger. "That's great news, isn't it, Mia?" She turned toward the girl. "You must feel incredibly relieved."

Mia looked somewhat dazed as she nodded. "He lucked out big time," she said.

"Could you direct us to the main office?" Officer Vargo asked. "We need to talk to the owner and start questioning the staff."

Ned pointed them in the direction of Mrs. McVee's office. "We want her to get word to all the guests that no one is to leave until everyone's been questioned," the detective said.

"Can we still leave to visit Michael?" Nancy asked.

"I don't see any problem with that," the detective said, "as long as you're back in an hour or so." With that, the two men headed down the corridor.

Nancy looked around. "Where's Mia?"

Ned frowned. "I don't know. I thought I heard her mumble something about needing to sit down, but I could be wrong."

"That would make sense," Nancy said. "Let's look for her."

Nancy and Ned made a thorough search of the inn and grounds but were unable to find Mia. Nancy took one last look in the parlor and saw Detective Dean speaking with Olivia. Nancy was turning away when she overheard the question the detective was asking.

"The night of the incident, did you see anybody in the kitchen during the time before the tea tray was brought out to the dining room?"

Nancy took a step closer.

"Well, there was the kitchen staff, of course, and Mrs. McVee and Jim Haines," Olivia said, pondering. "Oh, and I saw two of the guests, blond girls, who were in there at different times. I keep getting them mixed up when I make the rounds during our performances," she added with a sheepish smile. "Embarrassing!"

Detective Dean was jotting some notes in his book, when Nancy said, "Excuse me, Olivia, you say you saw *two* blond girls in the kitchen that night? I understood from Mrs. Wendham that only Trish was in there."

"Well, I guess she saw what she saw, but I definitely noticed both girls in there because I remember trying to keep them straight so that I could make my interactions with the guests more personal when I—"

"Thanks!" Nancy called over her shoulder as she bolted out of the room and up the stairs. She pounded on Mia's door but got no answer. She ran back down to the lobby, where Ned was just coming in from outside.

"No luck?" she asked.

Ned shook his head.

"Listen, Ned. Mia's not around, and I have reason to believe she might have been the one who poisoned Michael."

"What in the world—"

"I'll explain later," she said hastily. "Right now we need to call Michael at the hospital." Nancy picked up the phone at the vacant front desk.

"No dial tone," she said, alarmed. She pressed the buttons again and again, but got no response.

Ned saw Mrs. McVee coming out of her office. "Mrs. McVee, do you know how long the phones have been out?" he asked.

"Oh, all morning, unfortunately. A repairman is on his way over. Most inconvenient. I hope you haven't been troubled. Too much going on," she muttered, as she continued on down the hall.

"So Mia was lying about getting another threatening phone call," Nancy said, looking gravely at Ned. "I think I know where she went, and she's got a good head start on us. We need to get over to the hospital right now! And we should tell Detective Dean or Officer Vargo."

Ned took a quick look in the parlor, but didn't see the detective. He saw Trish coming in from outside and asked her to find either the detective or the police officer and tell them to get over to the hospital immediately. Then Ned and Nancy rushed out the door, leaving a bewildered Trish in the lobby. They jumped in the car and took off.

Nancy drove as fast as she could along the roads they'd found to be so dangerous the night before.

"Hurry, Nancy!" Ned exclaimed.

"We won't do Michael any good if we're DOA when we get there," Nancy said. "I'm driving as fast as I can."

"Sorry. You're right, Nan. I'm really anxious. I don't know why Mia has it in for Michael, but we have got to get there in time to stop her if she's working on her next move."

"I just hope we're not too late," Nancy said grimly.

A few minutes later, she screeched to a stop outside the hospital entrance. She and Ned jumped out, raced through the double doors, and ran on to the elevator just as the door was closing. On the third floor, they pounded down the corridor to Michael's room, astonished-looking nurses and orderlies jumping out of their way. Nancy burst into the room. Empty!

Nancy looked down the corridor and pointed at one of the nursing staff. "Quick, this is an emergency!" she cried. "Where is the patient who was in this room yesterday?"

The nurse stammered, looking confused.

"Please, think!" shouted Nancy.

"Uh, Room Four-fifteen, just up those stairs,"

the nurse stammered. "Or there's the elevator," she called as Ned and Nancy bolted up the stairwell.

They raced down the fourth-floor corridor and threw open the door to the room. Michael was asleep, and Mia was bending over his body, holding a hypodermic needle poised above his neck!

Chapter
Fifteen

No!" Nancy shouted. She crossed the room in two strides and grabbed Mia's arm, trying to force her to release the hypodermic.

Mia crashed into the bedside table, sending the pitcher and water glass onto the floor. Nancy pounded Mia's hand against the wall until the girl opened her hand and the needle went spinning under the bed. Nancy and Ned managed to wrestle Mia to the floor. She thrashed around, wild-eyed, as they each held one arm pinned to the floor. Nancy couldn't believe how strong Mia was.

Michael was wide awake now, sitting up in bed and staring wide-eyed at the scene. "Mia? What's going on here?" he demanded.

"She was trying to kill you!" Ned shouted, breathing heavily from his efforts.

"No, I never intended to kill him," Mia said quickly. Michael stared at his girlfriend, astounded, just as Detective Dean and Officer Vargo rushed into the room, followed by Trish. The two men summed up the situation quickly, then pulled Mia up off the floor and held her firmly between them. Trish stood trembling by the door, her hand over her mouth in shock.

"I just wanted to be number one," Mia said, looking at Michael. "All these years I've been in your shadow at school. You've been first in the premed program since the beginning. I never had a chance at getting the top position with you around." She shifted her eyes to the rest of them. "Everything would have been fine if Nancy hadn't stuck her nose in where it didn't belong!"

"So you poisoned the milk," Nancy said. "You faked the phone calls so you wouldn't be suspected. After all, who would suspect a victim?"

"I didn't use enough poison to kill him," Mia said. "Just enough to put him out of commission for a while. After all, I wouldn't risk killing Olivia. What if she'd taken milk in her tea, too? I'm not a bad person," she said.

"And when you found out Michael would be well in a few days, you decided to finish the job," Nancy said quietly.

"I didn't have a choice," Mia said. "I thought I could keep poisoning him for the next couple of months. I figured everyone would think he had a recurring virus. But when the poison was discovered . . ."

"But you were his girlfriend!" Trish exclaimed. "How could you do it?"

"Being his girlfriend was the only way to get close enough to get what I needed. I wanted to be the best," Mia said. "I deserve it." She turned back to Michael. "You've always had it easy, Michael," she said, seething.

Officer Vargo and Detective Dean started to escort Mia out of the room. She struggled, trying to break free, and turned back to Michael. "My plan would have worked," she screamed, "if I had only killed you in the first place!" The men gripped her tightly and dragged her out of the room.

Michael started pulling himself out of bed, and Ned rushed over to make sure he stayed put. Immediately, a nurse came into the room to check on Michael.

"Whew!" Nancy said. "That was close!"

"Too close," Ned agreed.

When the nurse was assured that Michael was okay, she left. Trish came over to the bedside, her face showing her concern.

"That was quite a scene," Michael said weakly. "I would never have guessed that Mia would do anything to hurt me."

"I didn't trust her from the start," Trish said. "She must have tried to set me up with that label you found," she said to Nancy. "And I know she exaggerated my phone calls to Michael to look like harassment."

"She set up Jim Haines, too," Nancy said. "She must have overheard me talking about the case with Ned. I guess she was covering all bases. She had this thought out long before the weekend," she added.

"She did know all the plans for the murder mystery weekend," Michael said. "I think I told you—it was her idea in the first place. We even came up several weeks ago to check the place out. And she knew I'd begged to be the first victim. What a joke that turned out to be." He gave a weak laugh.

"All she had to do was poison the milk in the pitcher," Nancy said to Michael. "She told us you weren't feeling well that day so we would think you just had the flu. Then when she realized I suspected you had been poisoned, she tried to make herself look like a victim by faking the phone calls. While everyone was worrying about her safety, she was off incriminating Trish and Jim, using the master keys. She could get into any room with those. She even got into my room," Nancy told Michael, "and used my lipstick to scrawl a threatening message on the mirror."

"She really had me fooled," Michael said.

"Don't feel bad," Nancy said. "She fooled me, too."

"Speaking of being fooled—or should I say

not being fooled," Ned spoke up, "I think I may know who the murderer is in the mystery play!"

"Oh, really?" Michael said. "So the great Ned Nickerson is on the case?"

Ned grinned. "Not great," he said. "Merely capable."

"If he does say so himself," Nancy said.

Ned laughed. "And we'd better get back," he said, "if I'm going to win the prize!"

"I'm going to stay a while longer," Trish said, "if that's okay with Michael."

"Sure it is, Trish," he told her. "We have some talking to do."

Nancy and Ned said their goodbyes. "Looks like they'll be able to mend their friendship," Nancy said as they left the hospital.

"That's not the only good news," Ned said when they reached the car. "You didn't get a ticket for parking illegally." They laughed, and he opened the passenger side door for Nancy.

"Hey, last time you were behind the wheel, we got driven off the road, remember?" she said.

"Just lean back and enjoy the ride," he said. "Nothing to worry about."

They arrived at the inn just as Detective Ryan was herding people into the library.

Matt saw Nancy and Ned and waved them over. "Come on, you guys, you're going to miss the last scene!"

Ned looked at Nancy and grinned. "Just in time!" he said. They followed the others.

The actors had gathered chairs around the large study table at one end of the room. The guests filed in and sat on the chairs and couches around the room. Once they were filled, the remaining guests stood, some leaning against the dark paneled walls.

Ned and Nancy were sitting near the front. "This is so cool," Ned said. "I wonder what my prize will be," he said.

Nancy rolled her eyes and smiled.

Detective Ryan started speaking. "We are here today to identify a thief and a murderer. For the past two days, the police have considered all relevant information and pieces of evidence. Now we are ready to announce our findings—"

"Only one person around this table had the motive, means, and opportunity to kill both Michael and Derek," Olivia said, interrupting the detective. She looked directly at Robert. "We all know who did it!"

"Only one of us has all the dirt on the Wendham family," Robert retorted. "Why not ask Jeffrey, the trusted family retainer, where the diamond necklace is!"

"Just be quiet!" the detective bellowed. "I've had enough of your outbursts!" They settled down.

"We have these pieces of evidence," he continued, pointing to the contents of a box on the table. "They suggest any number of motives."

The players started shouting again.

"That's enough!" the detective said. "One of you at this table is guilty." He looked around the room and addressed the guests. "You all have learned as much as the police have in this case. Can any among you name the murderer and reclaim the diamonds?"

A dark-haired girl by the window raised her hand. "The butler did it!" she stated. "He always does."

"Terribly sorry, my dear girl," Jeffrey said calmly, "Not in this case, I'm afraid."

"Anyone else?" Detective Ryan asked.

"I know!" Ned shouted. He stood up quickly and stepped over to the table.

"Well?" the detective demanded.

"The murderer and the thief are the same person. And that person is—" Ned paused dramatically, then turned and pointed. "Mickey Sloan!"

Mickey's hands flew to her mouth in surprise. "You're right. I did it, I did it!" she cried.

Detective Ryan clapped Ned on the back. "Good work!" he said heartily. "How did you know?"

"Well," Ned began, obviously relishing the spotlight, "just before he keeled over, Michael gave Olivia an obituary. And by the way, you all should know that the real Michael is going to be up and around in a couple days." That got a round of applause.

"The obituary, we learned, was for a woman

named Roseann Harriman Long, pictured in the paper as a young woman wearing diamonds. Olivia showed the obituary only to Derek Waverly, who was later killed, as was Olivia's fiancé, for knowing that piece of information. Those of us who carried Waverly up the lawn recall the death scene all too well," he added, rubbing his lower back. A few of the boys laughed at that, and a fully alive Derek Waverly waved from the back of the room.

"Okay, next we learned from Jeffrey that the Wendham family has some skeletons in the closet. And Mickey was obviously emotional about the secret she said she knew about Mrs. Wendham, making me think she had more than a gossip columnist's interest in the matter. That got me thinking about how very similar Olivia and Mickey are in appearance, with their green eyes and red hair. So I asked them each if their coloring was natural, and they both insisted they were natural redheads and didn't wear cosmetic contact lenses. So I figured they were related. Sisters? Cousins? But then where would the dead woman from the obituary fit in?"

"You need to get out more, Nickerson!" Matt shouted. "Where'd you find time to think up all this stuff?" Everybody laughed.

"Then there was the evidence in the rooms." Ned slid the box over, and pulled out a hacksaw. "From Mickey's room," he said. "Derek fell through a sawed railing at the gazebo. Mickey knew that Derek couldn't swim because she overheard Olivia making fun of him." Next Ned pulled out a piece of paper. "The note in Jeffrey's room warning the butler to keep what he knew to himself. This was just more evidence that the case involved some secret about the Wendham family. The insurance policy in Katherine Wendham's room," he said, holding it up. "This threw a little suspicion onto her, but hey, if she needed the money, why fake a theft when she could sell the diamonds a lot more easily? Finally, there was that lipstick message on Olivia's mirror. That was just to scare Olivia and encourage her to press her mother for family details, I think."

He looked at Mickey, and she nodded.

"Next I simply asked Mrs. Wendham if she was an only child, which she was not, and whether her maiden name had been Harriman, like the dead woman's. And the answer was yes. Right, Mrs. Wendham?"

The actress smiled and nodded.

"Okay. Then we found out from Mickey that Sloan wasn't her real name. I wanted to confirm that her name was really Harriman, but I didn't want Nancy to pick up my train of thought! Finally, I asked Mickey whether her mother was still alive, and she said—everybody all together, now . . ."

The audience joined him, shouting, "No!"

"So now I knew everything I needed to know. All that business in the scene between Mickey and Derek about Mickey only getting what was rightfully hers tipped me off and made me remember the diamonds pictured in the obituary. Then I guessed that she wanted the diamonds that had belonged to her mother, Katherine's sister, and that she would stop at nothing to have them. Right?" he asked, turning to Mickey.

Mickey stood up. "That's right. What you couldn't have figured out is that my mother married for love, not money, just like Olivia wanted to do." At this, Robert hung his head. "The family disowned her and took back everything, including those diamonds. She never wanted anything to do with the Wendham name, and neither did I. But when she died, I wanted to avenge her and to bury her wearing what was rightfully hers. I stole the diamonds and was safe until that sneak Michael showed up with the newspaper clipping. Of course I had to kill him—and Derek too, for getting too close to the truth.

"But I got what I wanted." Mickey smiled gently. "The diamonds are where they should be—with my mother."

A voice from the back of the room called out, "What about the blackmail? Who was blackmailing Derek?"

Jeffrey cleared his throat. "Mickey's not the only one who knew about Derek embezzling funds from the Wendham company. You don't suppose I was planning to finance my cruise with just my meager earnings, do you? Every butler needs an alternative source of income."

"And every case needs a red herring," Ned said, grinning. "This case is closed."

Mrs. McVee stepped into the middle of the room. "Congratulations!" she said, handing Ned an envelope. With that, everyone got up and started leaving the library. Ned shook hands with the actors, and Nancy saw him laugh as Olivia pulled off a natural-looking red wig.

At the final reception before heading home, Ned's friends crowded around, congratulating him. Jim Haines stepped close to Ned.

"Congratulations," Jim said, awkwardly shaking hands. "Sorry for all the hostility." He looked first at Ned, then at Nancy. "I know I need to learn to lighten up. No hard feelings?"

"No way, Jim," Ned said. "I'm sorry, too. Hey, we'll see you back at campus, right?"

Nancy filled two glasses with punch and gave a glass to Ned. "To the winner!" she said, and raised her glass. Everybody joined in a toast.

"Really, Ned," one of the guys said. "You got Nancy to help you, didn't you? That was phenomenal sleuthing!"

Ned shook his head. "No, I didn't," he said. "Nancy was too busy with her own case."

Nancy filled them in on her suspicions that Michael had been poisoned. She briefly told them about her investigation and then what had happened at the hospital. "So you see," she finished, "I didn't have time to help Ned."

"Now that we've nailed both cases, we could open up a detective agency together," Ned said. "Nickerson and Drew."

"That's Drew and Nickerson, isn't it?" Nancy retorted.

Ned laughed and reached into his jeans pocket. He pulled out the envelope containing his prize. "I never even checked out what I won!"

As they all waited, Ned ripped open the envelope and read the contents. "Oh, no!" he moaned.

"What's wrong?" Nancy asked.

"I won a certificate for another murder mystery weekend at the inn."

"That's great!" one of the guys said.

Ned smiled. "Not really," he said. "With Nancy around, I don't have to come to the inn to see mysteries—I live them!"